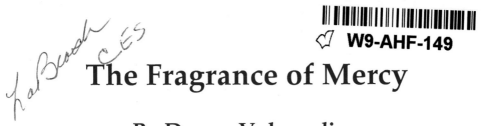

The Fragrance of Mercy

By Donna Volmerding

This book was written
to honor and serve
the TRIUNE GOD,
the One Who was, and is
and will be forever.

Acknowledgements

Thanks go to M.R., Lisa, Blake, Jeanie, David, Dennis, Lance, Phil, Chip, Brad, Tom and Gloria for your support and encouragement.

Kate O'Riordan's father Patrick, a newspaper reporter, was investigating a rape and possible murder in Vietnam that may have been committed by some in Charlie Company. Then Patrick dies in what was termed a tragic accident. Years later, Kate continues the investigation and one of her father's former Army buddies is murdered.

Will the killer(s) come to justice and at what cost? Will Kate be able to restore the shattered pieces of her life?

Chapter One
July 1983

Fort Summit, Indiana

Investigative reporter Patrick O'Riordan wasn't an easily frightened man. Years stepping in and out of people's lives had shown him both the best and the worst of humanity, and he carried no illusions of the evil inherent in the human heart. But tonight it wasn't someone else's life story passing before his eyes — it was his.

When he left the office, the sun was a sliver of orange that soon deserted the night sky. Thirty minutes later, it was too dark to decipher the color, make or driver of the vehicle that had been following him shortly after he reached the northern outskirts of Fort Summit.

As he rounded an unlit curve along the two-lane stretch of State Road 3 that rimmed the muddy St. Jude River, Patrick saw the size and span of those headlights, its steely-eyed beams glaring into his rearview mirror. Unknown to Patrick, they were a portent of danger. The vehicle sped rapidly close to his car, its lights blazing with blinding intensity. Now within inches of his Corolla, the menacing vehicle pounded Patrick's rear bumper with a powerful jolt, again and again, repeatedly causing his body to jerk spasmodically — forward and backward — each time it struck. Coldness gripped his heart with pulsing waves of fear.

The truck veered to the left of Patrick's car, pressing a wedge between the Corolla and the road's rocky descent on the right. Patrick realized in horror that his car was being forced off the road. To his passenger side was a craggy precipice bounded by a metal abutment and — deep, surging water.

He jerked his front wheels, hard, to the left, trying to push the weighty truck into the granite boulders on the opposite side of the road, but the truck's massive size dominated. The screaming of metal on metal, rock shearing steel and splintering glass filled his confused, frightened mind.

Frantically trying to understand, Patrick clutched at the thought of his daughter, Katie. *She was motherless and now, would she be fatherless, too? Why would anyone want to kill me?*

Grasping the wheel with both hands, his knuckles taut and white, he worked to stop the insistent force that lodged itself next to his car, aware of the imminent danger of the steep, rough-hewn drop-off. *Please, God, for Katie's sake, protect me.*

The truck was tenacious, jarring and jostling the Corolla harder to the right, running head to head with the skidding car, now so close to the edge of the rocky ridge his back end wrenched against the abutment, shattering his taillight.

Glass and rock and metal clawed and hissed and scratched while images of eternity and his beloved daughter and his dead wife fought for room in his mind. *Dearest Jesus, please help me! Please, for Katie's sake!*

He and his Goliath foe jerked and wrenched for every millimeter of road, splattering rocks and mud into the inkwell of the night. Beads of sweat dripped into Patrick's eyes; he kneaded them with a tight fist as his right hand held fast to the wheel.

Think, he told himself. *Just hold your own. I've been in worse than this.*

In a hundred yards, the road cut to the left, veering at a 45-degree angle toward a bridge that crossed the rushing water.

Hold your ground; reach the bridge; you can make it. Start braking before you get to the bridge. Careful not to crash into it — or hit the rail guarding the road's end. Steady now; don't give an inch. Now brake, hard!

Patrick saw an eerie scene transfixed in slow-motion video — the truck forcing his car too far to the right, his Toyota fishtailing on the gravel shoulder, smashing into the sidewall before the bridge, then rolling and hurtling in its airborne trajectory into the black depths of oblivion, into the inky, roiling rapids of the St. Jude River.

The truck's fender smashed the inside bridge wall, its taillights careening as it righted itself and screamed on its way.

Patrick's last prayer was *Father, into Thy hands I commit my spirit.*

• • •

June 1983 — one month earlier

The day dawned with bright hues of purple, red and fluorescent gold as Patrick O'Riordan drove to his office at The Fort Observer. On these glorious June mornings, his mind basked in the warm memories of his childhood. They hearkened a young barefoot boy, visiting grandparents at their lake cottage on Lake Serene in northern Indiana. And he would never forget the cool sensation of oozy mud between his toes, the squishy feel of bee moths on a hook, the gentle encouragement of his grandfather, the soft skin on his grandmother's face when she tenderly hugged him.

His cheek was still sticky with the strawberry jelly his daughter had slathered on toast before giving him a wet good-bye kiss. Katie, who had just turned six, was his only child. Her mother, Emily, died of an abdominal aneurysm shortly after giving birth.

At first after his wife's death Patrick questioned the equity of a universe that would permit such a crushing blow. He tried to understand, rationally, why a loving God would allow such violence and chaos in a world He created to be peaceful and ordered.

After awhile, the pain was not as sharp. It would never go away, of course, but it was different. The memories, though clear as ever, no longer stabbed his gut with the wrenching heaves of loneliness, abandonment and loss as they did in those first days, weeks, months after Emily's death.

In the process of grieving, guilt and anger may be the hardest aspects to reconcile. Patrick knew his marriage was solid, happy, committed, but sometimes his mind would torment him with the silly arguments, the overextended work hours, the sacrifices made during the "poor" years.

Other times he would rail against a perverse God Who would allow such anguish to be brought on those He claims to love so deeply. Grief is a complicated process, he learned, not given to easy answers, glib words, superficial advice; those empty sayings are Pollyanna nonsense. Grief is a concentrated jumble of all the wonderful, difficult, glorious, hurtful, funny, morose, carefree, tense remembrances of one deeply loved and greatly missed. It is a process that never ends, although, with time, joyful memories heighten like waves on the sea as sorrow recedes in the undertow of regret.

Patrick chose to remember his wife's sweet giggly laugh that heralded the sun regardless of weather, the gentle strokes and soft kisses that radiated his body, the curve of her leg, the insouciance of a head toss in a brisk breeze.

He would never understand why his wife died, although he was stuck on that question for some time before finding acceptance. God had put him and his daughter in this situation, and God would get them through it.

• • •

Patrick was a handsome man who stood six feet tall with a naturally lean and athletic body. His thick, sandy-blond hair would occasionally tumble down his forehead, and he would quickly brush the straight, errant strand with a comb of his fingers. He used to play the guitar but had not pursued it in years. Mostly, he was a writer, one gifted in style and insights who had dedicated his life to telling the truth in an unvarnished, concise manner.

He wasn't particularly complicated. He was impatient with whiners, grumblers and those given to '60s existential angst. He would mock them by placing the back of his hand over his forehead, rolling his eyes heavenward, and declaring with a grand flourish, "Oh, what is the meaning of life?"

He would not engage in such narcissistic musings. No, Patrick was a straight-up kind of guy who brooked no nonsense, with a conscience as razor sharp as a bacon slicer.

As managing editor for The Fort Observer, a mid-size morning publication based in Fort Summit, Indiana, Patrick's life had reached a certain level of professional and private accomplishment. Rumors had it that he was in place to be the next executive editor for the paper, whenever Joe Randolph, the present executive editor, either left for Washington D.C. as senator or took over the corporate reins of his father's company.

• • •

The telephone call came about 10:00 a.m., just after

10

Patrick refilled his coffee cup for the third time.

"Hey, Riordan, you still like tan coffee?" came the voice.

Patrick recognized who it was immediately but not by the voice. Only one person, Tom Becker, dropped the "O" from his last name and teased him relentlessly about his coffee preference.

Tom, Patrick and Joe were Army buddies in Vietnam — Charlie Company, reconnaissance 29th combat brigade. They fought together, joked together, became fast friends and kiddingly called themselves "the three." But the close relationship Patrick and Tom shared in wartime could not sustain itself through distance, family and work pressures.

Patrick and Joe returned to hometown roots; Tom chose the corporate life in Chicago. They tried to keep in touch, at first through frequent phone calls that became less regular over the years. They exchanged Christmas cards and even had yearly visits, for a while. Patrick blamed himself for the distance between them and vowed to do better in the future.

"Becker! You still searching for your soul mate?" he laughed. After three wives, and three divorces, Tom's marital history was a source of levity.

His voice was so whispered, Patrick had difficulty hearing him.

"I'm staying at the Holiday Inn here. Could we talk?"

Just then, Joe Randolph knocked twice at Patrick's open office door but didn't wait for a "come in." He didn't have to. He was the paper's executive editor and the heir apparent to his father's corporation, of which the paper was one medium-sized asset.

"I'm looking for the files on the Debeney article," he whispered, noticing Patrick's hand cradling the phone. Patrick pointed to a dented file cabinet.

"Joe's here, Becker. You want to give him some grief, too?"

"Don't tell him I'm here in town," Tom rasped. His cavalier tone turned dark. Patrick stumbled on his words, then recovered quickly.

"Wha-? I know, you're too cheap to pay for a chatty long-distance phone call. Hey, Joe, Becker says 'hi.' He says he can't talk long, he's late for a meeting, but he'll catch ya later."

Joe smiled understandingly, held the Debeney file up to show he retrieved it, then left the room with a quick step, his long legs in a slow jog.

"What's going on?" Patrick said.

"Listen, I have something I want to tell you and only you. Can we meet someplace tonight? Somewhere that's not frequently attended by people you know?"

"Sure. What time?"

• • •

Patrick waited in the parking lot outside Billy's, a bar outside of town where the food is greasy and the women are tart. Although the lot had some gravel stones in it, they were inadequate coverage for the mud holes and tire spins from several too-fast exits and grandstanding doughnuts. The weeds were so plentiful the lot appeared to be a fuzzy green, with an occasional speckle of road stone quilted among the dandelions and the ooze.

Tom pulled up in a red '82 Triumph TR7 Cabriolet with its top down, a jaunty little number for a newly single man. By contrast, its driver appeared exhausted. His formerly full head of hair was largely gone, with only a few aberrant patches on the back of his head. His complexion was rosy, as if he'd been burned by the sun, but it wasn't a healthy glow. He'd put on some pounds, and his face was swollen. His unsteady walk was a sure giveaway; he was not well.

Patrick embraced him, and Tom lingered a bit too long. The two entered the bar under a red neon sign that glowered c-ld beer; hot fo-d.

Blue billows of smoke hung in the air like low-lying clouds, exuding a thin film that deadened colors and gave the cheap candles a hazy glow. Country music blared in the next room, where a few beer-tippled folks with oversized cowboy hats hoofed the line dance.

Boozy tittering and loud voices were everywhere around them. The women ratted and profusely sprayed their hair; their excessive make-up and fire-truck red lipstick were a gaudy complement to tight, revealing clothing stretched over ample bodies. Age and extra pounds rendered their appearance garish and hard, women desperately grasping to be young, though youth had not been kind to them.

13

The men were just as needy. With oversized stomachs and undersized wallets, they were looking for a steamy night with lithe, long-legged babes, or settle for women with a mother complex and a hefty bank balance who would just take care of them.

No one recognized the two men as they huddled together in deep discussion in a back table of the bar. Patrick listened intently and hugged his beer bottle with both hands. Tom nervously gulped his beer and bit into a handful of potato chips.

"Riordan, I'm a dying man. It started with prostate cancer; the docs said it went undetected for too long, and it's spread. I have three tumors in my brain. The radiation therapy is keeping them at bay for a while, but I know I have only three, maybe four months to live."

Patrick felt as if he had been kicked in the stomach and was struggling for breath. His mind was going in a hundred directions, but he just wanted to find the right words to say, the correct phrase that would salve this gaping wound.

"I'm really sorry, man," he stammered. "Is there anything I can do?"

Tom's gray eyes were tired, but they demonstrated a steely determination that Patrick witnessed in Vietnam.

"Yes, there is. Oh, there's nothing you can do for me," he said with a dismissive wave of his formerly chip-filled hand, "but I want you to right a wrong, a wrong that has haunted me since Vietnam."

14

"I'm listening."

Tom stared into Patrick's eyes as his tongue lodged itself into the side of his mouth. Then his gaze veered downward.

"It was in the fall of '69, October 23rd, when we were camped near Vinh Long. There was a small village to the north of us, and some of the guys heard that Vietcong were hiding there. They figured they could flush them out more easily at night in a surprise attack."

Patrick remembered well; after that night, things were never the same in C Company. A pall was cast over the camaraderie that formerly existed between the men who shared food, laughter and their deepest fears. Of the five who went — Tom, Joe, Ralph Sherman, Rick Schmidt and Larry Anders — none returned from that night expedition the same. They were sullen and terse when asked about it.

The rumor was that something terrible happened that night, something more than flushing out the enemy, but no one who went would ever speak of it again. It was as if the entire incident was erased from their memory, and they only wanted to believe they spent the night playing poker.

"You didn't go because you hurt your foot," Tom remembered. "Pete Fogel had dysentery, and Steve Westoff stayed back to watch the camp. Capt. Peterson put Steve in charge for the night. Cap was meeting with other officers."

Tom filled his chubby hands with several more chips,

15

taking bites of each one as he talked. He took another long pull from his beer, then wiped his lips with the back of his hand.

"We didn't encounter any Vietcong that night, but we came upon a young couple who were screwing around. When the boy saw five American soldiers, armed to the teeth, he ran as fast as a cheetah. The rest of us …" Tom's gaze fell on his beer. He quickly swilled the rest of it and ordered another.

"The rest of us …" His eyes glistened in the hazy glow as he haltingly continued, "raped her." The last two words were said so softly that Patrick could barely hear them.

Tom rubbed his forehead with his fingers, back and forth and back again, as if to wipe away fourteen years of guilt that had eaten at his heart as surely as this cancer was killing the rest of him.

"I know what I did — what we did — was wrong," he blurted. "I-I know it was …" His voice trailed off.

Patrick remained silent, squirming in his seat, searching Tom's face for explanation. He loved these guys, all of them, and his heart broke at the prospect of receiving such devastating news.

"There's more," Tom's voice quavered. "I can't die with this on my conscience, Riordan." He closed his eyes tightly in a vain effort to fight back tears and put it all behind him.

"We knew we couldn't leave the girl alive. She'd go back to her village and talk. We panicked. So we

16

decided to draw cards; you remember Joe always had a deck on him. Whoever drew the ace of spades had to ..." Falteringly, he searched for the words to explain the evil, bloody act as old as Cain's, "had to silence her permanently."

"Are you certain the girl was killed?"

"One of the villagers found the body the next day. Someone knew the boy was with her, so he was the one who took the blame. I heard the girl's father ended up killing the boy, to protect his daughter's honor."

A single tear trailed down Tom's face, winding its way to the lower side of his cheek before his right index finger held it there, his hand moving slowly upwards, pushing it so hard against the skin he creased his eye.

"I don't know who drew the card; I just know I didn't. And maybe the boy did end up killing her, but I doubt it."

A woman screeched a giddy peal of liquored laughter as the discordant strains of squealing guitars mocked the smoky room filled with sweat and booze and strong perfume. But for Patrick, the deadened silence between the two men was as numb and lifeless as the feeling in his heart.

Tom broke the silence when his beer arrived.

"You're a reporter, Riordan, a damn good one, and I want you to find out about this."

Both calculated the soldiers in Charlie Company, who lost their way that fateful night and forever seared their consciences — Larry Anders, Ralph Sherman, Joe

17

Randolph and Rick Schmidt.

"I assume the other three men are still alive," Patrick mused.

"I think so. Here's the phone numbers and addresses for Rick and Larry. I still don't have Ralph's. I should have that information to you before, well ..."

Patrick's voice trailed off. The two nervously chugged their beers, casting their eyes on the soft pine table, its nicks and scratches the result of hard use and ill treatment.

"I make no promise, Tom, but I'll do the best I can."

"I know you will. That's why I asked you."

Chapter Two

To Patrick, his tour in Vietnam felt as if hopelessness covered those who dared to enter its borders like a widow's veil, an abandonment by God or luck or all the forces of good that weighed as heavily on the troops as an iron sheath. The suffocating heat of that miserable land, so fraught with war, and hate, and bloodshed, even the moist earth seemed to stink of sweat and blood and futility itself. It was endemic in the air, in the soil, in every molecule of water that mingled with the tears of those who inhabited this wretched place. And let all who enter its desolate gates be wary; hope and goodness must be checked at the door. Things changed in Vietnam, men changed, hearts changed, he reflected. What was right was turned on its head; what was wrong, well, what is wrong? And for that matter, what is right?

• • •

October 23, 1969 — Vinh Long, Vietnam

The young girl lay naked on the prickly leaves, bleeding and hurt, with her hands tied to a wild rubber tree. Her boyfriend had long disappeared, and she hoped that the American soldiers who raped her were gone, too. But she heard the rustle of footsteps coming toward her, and she saw the uniform of an American soldier approaching. Fear and panic overwhelmed her, and she tried to scream, but the handkerchief stuffed into her mouth muffled her noise. The silent figure paused, touched her wrist, cut her ties, then faded into the night. She was bleeding profusely and could barely get up, limping, treading the sodden earth, when she felt a strong arm envelop her and another arm snap her neck. This would be the last night of life for Phi Nhung Nguyen.

• • •

Patrick's uneasy sleep was filled with fitful dreams of cold-eyed soldiers in a murderous assault on a young life. Raping this young woman, using her body like a dime-store mannequin, a doll built for the pleasure of men with lascivious hearts and puerile minds, then murdering her, abandoning her young life in the belly of that God-forsaken earth played out the karma of this land.

The bitter reality of this grisly scene was made even more pungent when Patrick pictured his daughter, more precious than air, being hurt in any way. He shuddered that something so unthinkable could ever happen to his Katie, the heart of his life. After the death of his wife, Katie was his reason for grasping at the raft of life and not allowing depression to suck him under in a maelstrom that had no passage out. He felt as if he were a rat on a wheel, ingesting daily doses of gloom and despair, with aching loneliness as a chaser. But each morning and every night, he listened to the music of his daughter's cooing burbles, enchanted by the little smile that crinkled the sides of her delicate nose.

She was a sweet-natured baby who matured into a toddler with unbounded energy. She took her first steps at eight months; she ran at nine months. Perhaps the only trait more bountiful than her high vitality was an unstoppable curiosity that matched that of her father. She loved to be read to, even as a small baby, and Patrick would often find Katie in her crib, looking at the pictures in the books, completely absorbed in their fascinating world.

By the age of two-and-a-half, Katie was speaking in complete sentences and expressing herself on the level of three- and four-year-olds. One of her first words was not the common "da-da," it was "dah-dee," with an emphasis placed on the "dee." Once, when he was bathing her, she exclaimed, "Know what, dah-dee? You're ni-ice." It was especially endearing because "ni-ice," a monosyllabic word pronounced as two syllables, was given a tonal upturn on the last part that resonated almost as a question. "You're ni-ice," that simple exclamation by his blond-haired little girl, her blue eyes melting his broken heart like a waxen shell that came too close to a flame, would carry him through many bleak nights and dismal days. The smallest kindness from the love of his life melded with his splintered spirit.

Although Patrick's parents loved Katie as a daughter, and became the primary caretakers while he was at work, he vowed to take on nothing more that would fill his otherwise empty life. This tow-headed little cherub had had the ill-fated fortune to lose her mother; he would not sacrifice her father, too.

Wherever Patrick went, other than the office, Katie was in his arms or holding his hand with tender firmness. She was his ubiquitous shadow at the grocery, the drugstore, the ice cream parlor. It was she who chose the freshest fruit, the firmest snap beans, the right shape of pasta.

Perhaps out of pity for this motherless child, "Dutch" at the drugstore always had a sucker or a foil-wrapped sweet for Patrick's little girl. Others performed thoughtful gestures, too. Compliments, warm hellos, extra tickets to a G-rated movie, books laid aside at the library for Katie's edification, or a cluster of golden mums brought to the house as a good-luck measure for her first day of kindergarten were common occurrences.

Patrick took to fathering with such focused devotion he even surprised himself. Before Katie's birth, he and his wife, Emily, marked with pleasure the change of her body, the little kicks in her extended abdomen, the arm or leg that traveled across her swollen belly from one side to another, and sometimes back again.

He always knew he wanted to be a father, and, though his excitement was tempered with sober concern about supporting and rearing this young life, he cherished the thought of finally introducing himself to this precious stranger.

How would he go about doing that, he wondered. Would he just play it straight up, look into those newborn liquid eyes and say, "Hi, I'm your father"? Or should he be coy, wait his turn, let others have the opportunity to meet this much-anticipated baby? He figured when the time came, he would know what to do.

He was certain, of course, that he would love his child. But he did not understand, and who could understand before becoming a parent, the ineffable love that a parent has for a child. The depth of his commitment, nurture, care and nonstop concern for this little life was a network of passion that penetrated his being so extensively, he often wondered if his heart could contain all that love.

Katie was more than the sun, the moon and the stars to him. That cliché didn't even register on Patrick's love scale. No, Katie was a billion universes, ten trillion moons and a hundred gazillion stars to her father. From the first nanosecond he held her, her little fuzzy pink blanket gently framing her perfectly shaped head with its little blonde wisps of down, his life, his love, his entire view of the world and life itself were unalterably changed.

• • •

He awoke early that morning; the clock on his nightstand registered 4:02. He tried to return to slumber, but no position, no matter how formerly comfortable, could calm his churning thoughts or check the anguishing pain in his heart. He knew that somewhere between the daily duties of his life and the cherished time spent with his daughter, he must seek out the truth

23

about this grisly incident, no matter what the consequences.

Patrick was a gifted reporter who had a deep need to know the full story and all the facts. A reporter, an exceptional reporter, doesn't always give the public all the information he, or she, has. Some of it could be libelous, some of it merely embarrassing but not germane to the story. Other information registers more on the gossip scale as whispered innuendoes that smear names, reputations and lifestyles.

Patrick was sensitive to certain information or situations that did not need to be reported publicly, but he wanted a full, behind-the-scenes accounting to settle his misgivings.

On the matter of the murder of an innocent teen fourteen years ago, Patrick didn't desire revenge or blood or payment. His need to know bore no vindictiveness, although his deep disillusionment was certainly a driving force that fueled his investigation. No, retaliation was not in the picture, but he hoped understanding and justice would come, even if it occurred later.

• • •

"Pat, did you hear me? I asked you what you thought of the Anderson piece."

"Oh, Sam, yeah, I did read it," Patrick said, turning his gaze away from the dirty window in his office. "I thought his points about downtown development were very promising."

"Is everything okay? You seem distant. You must have looked out that window for 10 minutes, but there's nothing to see but traffic."

Sam Owen was chief editorial writer and Patrick's good friend for the eight years Pat worked for The Fort Observer. His writing was crisp and insightful, and his direct, upfront manner appealed to Pat.

"I can't get anything past you, can I?" Patrick responded with a self-conscious chuckle. He weaved his fingers together and placed his chin on top of them. "I do have something on my mind, but I assure you, it's not a personal problem. It's just something I've got to do."

"Okay," Sam said, his eyes steadily examining Patrick's demeanor. "We'll run the article in Saturday's guest column. And, uh, if you ever need someone to just listen, I'm always here."

"Thanks. I may take you up on that offer."

• • •

Patrick was uncertain where to begin his investigation, but he decided to talk to Rick, then Larry. Patrick's boss Joe was campaigning for the U.S. Senate, a position that would thrust his political ambitions onto the national scene. His time was taken up with breakfast meetings, out-of-town rallies and $200-a-plate fundraisers. Opportunity would present itself to discuss this issue — but not right now.

Rick Schmidt had settled in Pass City, Ind., where his social skills were put to good use as a marketing executive and occasional salesman for Soy Green. Although not unattractive, Rick was no Adonis, either. He was average in height, about 5'10", and his formerly lean build had added about 25 pounds over the years. His features were pleasant enough, but his ordinary attributes disguised the charismatic smile and the warmth that glimmered through his brown eyes. Rick was a born salesman whose unaffected, sincere manner could charm the socks off a cold Eskimo.

• • •

Patrick's call came in the early afternoon, shortly after Rick finished a power lunch with a promising client. Rick was surprised to hear the voice of his former Army buddy.

"Patrick, it's so good to hear from you. How've you been?" It was a common question, but somehow, when Rick asked it, one had the impression he really did want to know.

The two had not been in touch for about nine years, just shortly after Katie was born. Rick called to express his sympathy, and the two had a brief conversation. Of course, Rick offered to help in any way he could, and Patrick fully intended to keep in touch, but time is a grinding machine that wears away at even the staunchest resolutions.

After Katie's birth and his wife's death, the days, weeks and even years following were a blur in Patrick's memory, with the daily duties of work and home and child becoming so overwhelming at times that he had to remind himself to eat.

"Things are going fine for me," Patrick said, "but I saw Tom Becker last night, and he's not doing well."

"Becker? You saw him last night?"

"Yeah, he came in for an evening and wanted to have a beer."

"What's wrong with him?"

"He has cancer, says he's terminal, and he looks awful."

"Gee, I'm sorry to hear that. Is he still married to, um, Nancy?"

"No, she was number two. Andrea was number three, but that only lasted eleven months."

"Wow, that guy gets around. Any kids?"

"No. There was a stepson with his first marriage, but I don't think they're close." An awkward pause punctuated the easy conversation. Patrick cleared his throat, then said, "Rick, there's something I need to talk to you about, something that Tom said happened in Vietnam, in October 1969. Do you remember the incident I'm referring to?"

The tone in Rick's voice tightened, his manner no longer breezily chatty. With hesitant, whispered undertones, he said, "I think so." Neither man said anything for several seconds, then Rick jumped in with a flourish of quick words, coupled together like a speeding train on a runaway track.

"Listen, Pat, that is a part of my past that I never want to go back to, never, do you understand? I have tried to forget it, really tried, and just when I think I've succeeded, something happens, and I relive the guilt and the anguish and the horror and, for God's sake, why would Tom even bring this up?"

Patrick paused briefly before calmly, deliberately, speaking.

"He said the incident haunts him to this day, and he doesn't want to die until some, well, some explanation has been made. Could we just meet somewhere and talk about it?"

"I want no one else to know, not my wife, not my kids. I'm serious, Pat, no one else must know."

"I understand, Rick. Look, I'm not trying to nail anyone. I'm not out for revenge. I just want some answers; I need to know what happened, everything you can tell me. I don't want to hurt you."

"I'll tell you what I know, all of it, but then I never want to discuss it again. Never. And I will not testify against anyone, or talk with the military about it. I'm sorry, Pat. I just can't do any more."

After the two decided on time and place, Patrick hung up the receiver with a sad insight into human character: These were five men whom he trusted with his life, joked with, slept with, played with, thought he knew to the inside of their soul — five men who raped an innocent life, and one of them bears the mark of Cain.

The vaunted nature of our better angels may be overrated, he assessed.

Chapter Three

Joe Randolph poked his head inside Patrick's office to remind him about tomorrow's early morning meeting with the staff.

"Hey, what's up?" he asked. "You look as forlorn as the horse who came in fourth. Anything I need to know about?"

"Uh, no, I've just been …, well, you know the call from Tom Becker?" Patrick looked at Joe's blank face, who creased his brow out of curiosity when Patrick paused. "He has terminal cancer," Patrick stumbled. "I guess I'm just really bummed about it."

Joe's mouth dropped wide open in a gesture of shock. He stared, nonplused, trying to grasp the cruel words — terminal cancer. His jaw closed around two words: "How long?"

"Tom thinks about three or four months."

Joe sucked in a deep breath, then exhaled quickly as his shoulders drooped about his collar. "That's really rough. I'll call him tonight."

"I think he would appreciate that." Patrick looked down at the ever-present pile of papers on his desk, then let his gaze meander back to Joe. "About that meeting — I'll, uh, see you tomorrow at seven."

• • •

Patrick and Rick met at a family restaurant in Maryville, about ten miles from Fort Summit, where farmers and their families are early to bed and early to rise.

Patrick arrived at the eatery first — his penchant for promptness was almost a handicap — and Rick entered wearing shorts and a knit shirt he'd bought on sale. It was, Patrick guessed, Rick's way of going incognito. No expensive suits or silk ties, no Ralph Lauren shirts or gold cuff links; someone may recognize him in his business attire. But wearing shorts, well, Rick had a face as common as sticks. It was the pricey extras that carried his professional bearing.

Although Rick was guarded, his naturally warm mannerisms drew people onto his team. He was a salesman, and not even the hint of a scandal could dampen his public demeanor.

"Look, Pat, I didn't mean to be rude to you over the phone. But, believe me, this whole mess has been awful. I have a good job, respect, a family. I have two daughters of my own."

His voice splintered off. Closing his eyes, he wedged his finger between his forehead and cheeks. He sighed deeply, then squeezed his temples in an effort to collect his composure. His embarrassment was evident in the strain of his eyes when he looked at Patrick.

"I just want to put it behind me, for good, forever."

"I understand that, Rick," Patrick said gently. "But a young girl has been murdered, and ..."

"I didn't do it," he said brusquely. "Look, we found this girl with her boyfriend. She obviously had been played before, and when he ran away, well, stuff happens."

Rick's eyes sparked with anger. "You remember how it was, Pat. Those people were untrustworthy. They'd strap bombs to kids to blow us up. We lost at least a dozen men, good men, to their buried explosives, and how many others lost limbs? I hated them, all of them, and I didn't think much about it with the girl, either. It wasn't until I got back home and had girls of my own that I realized what I'd done."

"What happened next?"

"Afterward, we knew we had a problem to take care of. The girl's wrists were tied to a tree, her mouth was stuffed with someone's hankie so she couldn't scream. I don't know who said what first. I just remember that Joe pulled out that damn deck of cards he always carried, and whoever got the ace of spades had to," his voice faltered, "had to take care of the problem.

"We agreed that no one would know who did it and that none of us would ever discuss it again. But there it was. The whole thing attached itself to our souls like a blood-sucking animal."

The emotion playing so strong in Rick's eyes that even constant blinking couldn't dispel the small, watery drop that edged its way down his right cheek and played itself around the corners of his mouth.

Knotting his fingers together, opening and closing them, Patrick drew his clenched hands to his upper lip.

"That leaves three others," he said, gazing at the

remains in his coffee cup. "Tell me what you did after the cards were dealt."

"We were ordered to take off in different directions, alone, before heading back to camp. When we got to camp, we were not allowed to let anyone else know we had arrived. That way, none of us would know who got the card."

"Who made the order?"

"I think it was Anders. Yeah, I'm pretty sure it was Anders. We used to kid him about having a Napoleon complex. He always liked to be in charge, often threatened to call his lawyer on someone if they didn't do things his way."

"Is there anything else you remember about that night? Even if it seems insignificant?"

"No. When I got to camp, I went straight to bed. I have no idea who was there and who was not."

• • •

Larry Anders, a short, scrawny man with a beaked nose and thin eyebrows, was reared on a farm near Baker, Ohio, about 30 miles east of Fort Summit. He took over its operation when his father became ill. A man of average intelligence and ability, Larry yearned for the respect of his peers, and the power and control that comes to those who generate the trust and admiration of others.

The fact that he lacked the seeds of greatness in any form certainly must have crossed his mind, but his fabricated ego, masking deep roots of inferiority, allowed him little insight and no wisdom about leadership. Often, his actions were a caricature of the humorous Barney Fife and his pompous posturing. Larry would yank his pants up from the back and sniff the air just before admonishing an underling. All that was missing in this scenario was the background music to Barney's puffed-up demeanor, that cadence of "da da da dee, da da da dum, da da da dee dee dum dee dum," just before he arrested a hazardous jaywalker or a menacing five-year-old stealing candy.

• • •

Patrick drove up the deeply rutted, partially graveled driveway to Larry's house and parked his Toyota beside a large, black pickup that was almost as muddy as the path from the road. He was met by a fleshier version of Mr. Fife. Larry's paunch hung over his jeans in a manner that caused the front half of his pants to rest lower, perpendicular with the horizontal hang of his stomach. This, in turn, appeared to draw the back of his pants at an even higher angle. At one point during their conversation, when Larry characteristically jerked at the back of his trousers and snorted in his inimical puffed-up manner, Patrick had to stifle a guffaw, despite the serious nature of this visit.

The farmhouse was a white two-story wood-framed structure, typical of houses that sprinkled the Ohio and Indiana landscapes. Its interior was clean and decorated in acceptable, safe colors and inexpensive furniture with plastic moldings that tried, and failed, to look upscale.

Larry's wife, Sharon, greeted the two at the door and led them into the living room. Sharon wore her medium-brown hair in a cropped, combed-back style that emphasized the plainness of her features. A gray knit top hung across her hunched shoulders, and she completed the ensemble with navy shorts and dirty white sneakers.

"Can I get you anything to drink?," she said in a manner as flat as the farmland that surrounded her.

"Nothing for me, thank you," Patrick responded.

"Yeah, I'd like a beer," Larry ordered. "Maybe you can bring some chips, too."

"So what is this all about?," Larry demanded, tightening his jaw. Crossing his arms in front of him, his eyes bored into Pat's. Patrick uncrossed his legs, then leaned forward a little in his chair, clasping his hands between his knees in a vain attempt to deflect Larry's stern gaze.

Patrick cleared his throat, looked down at the carpet, then drew a deep breath.

"I talked to Tom Becker the other day. He, uh, he's dying, from cancer, hasn't got long to live. Larry, he told me what happened in 'Nam the night of October 23, when you, Tom, Joe, Rick and Ralph scouted for Vietcong and came across that teen girl. Tom said —"

"I don't know what Tom told you, but I had nothing to do with any of that," Larry interrupted.

"You were there, weren't you?"

"Yeah, I was there, but —"

34

Larry stopped when he saw Sharon enter the room with his beer and a large metal bowl filled with chips. Sharon, sensing the awkwardness of the instant silence, smiled wanly and headed for her bedroom.

"I don't know what happened to that girl," he whispered, until Sharon was safely out of earshot. "As far as I know, she's married with 12 kids by now."

"Why don't you just tell me what you recall about that night — you know, who said what, who did what."

Larry widened his lips so thin they were a slash across his face. He shifted his weight and glanced sideways with a deep sigh.

"The five of us were scouting this village north of Vinh Long. We came across this slutty girl and her boyfriend. When he ran away, we took our frustrations out on her. We were just a bunch of goofy guys who did something stupid. Why are you dragging this up, anyway?"

"The girl was murdered."

"I don't know anything about that," Larry said. "Joe dealt some cards; he said whoever pulled the ace of spades had to deal with it. I figured someone threatened her if she said anything, then let her go."

"Someone made the order to have everyone scatter, then head back to camp incognito. Any idea who gave that order?"

Larry stuck his tongue in his cheek in a defiant gesture, then slowly rubbed his hands together, ponderously, before responding.

"Maybe I told everyone to leave by himself and head back to camp, but so what? I didn't do anything wrong."

"That remains to be seen," Patrick responded softly, avoiding Larry's vexed stare by looking at his shoe. "Whoever killed that young girl —"

"How do you know that? She may still be alive. Her death is only Tom's guess. No one saw anything, and probably no one did anything to hurt her. Case closed."

"Someone does know something, and that's what I'd like to find out," Patrick said as he lifted himself from the chair. "If there's any more information you can give me, I'd appreciate a call at this number."

"There ain't nothin' else," Larry said. "It happened a long time ago. I forgot about it."

"Yes, well, thank you for your time."

Patrick drove out of the furrowed driveway and passed the muddy fences that bordered a portion of Larry's pig farm, deep in thought about people's varied responses to pain, tragedy, even murder.

• • •

Large portions of Ohio, like Indiana, are agrarian, filled with acres of soybeans that reflect the golden June sun on their wind-kissed leaves; shocks of corn clamber for the sky, and an occasional horse lazily feeds on hay, its tail flicking away the irritating horseflies so abundant in these parts.

The squirrels are brown and even black in the Midwest, Patrick mused, unlike the grey ones that scamper on the East Coast. And that repugnant smell that instantly filled his lungs and caused him to scrunch his face, that is definitely a skunk, he thought, a dead skunk, as he replayed the line from Bob Dylan's song. There's a dead skunk in the middle of the road. This short bout of silliness was an oasis from the dark thoughts that dominated his mind the past week. Despite doubts, dark times and lots of life questions, there was an unsinkable optimism in Patrick, rooted in the conviction that those who choose the good, the right, the moral are the strongest people.

• • •

His levity was shortened by the clanging sound of a railroad crossing, its lights flashing warning.

"Dammit!" Patrick swore to himself. He was always in a rush to meet schedules and deadlines. He just didn't have time to wait for a long train, and this was a long one.

Realizing, once again, that his impatience needed to be tamed, he relaxed his posture and reminded himself to calm down; it's only a few minutes, he reasoned. Be still. This, too, shall pass.

• • •

Larry's cover-up frustrated Pat. Belligerence was as much a part of Larry's character as his annoying idiosyncrasies, and Patrick knew his guilt should not be assumed because of them. Rick had seemed truly remorseful for what had happened, but his smooth exterior could perhaps allay any suspicions of guilt. What about the other two — Ralph Sherman and Joe

Randolph?

Ralph Sherman, also of Charlie Company, had skin the shade of dark mahogany, stood 6'3", and, as a former college fullback for Indiana University, was built like a large armoire, with a neck as thick as a young woman's waist. His mellow personality was an easy mesh with Rick's outgoing assertiveness, and a comfortable fit with the rest of C Company. Ralph demanded no special attention, and his sense of humor was always a calming influence on the occasional hijinks of the men.

And then there was Joe. The son of a wealthy man, Joe worked hard at being one of the guys. He wasn't one to flaunt his privilege or brag about his cars or clothes nor "one up" anyone about his future acceptance to Harvard. Though quite intelligent, he was careful to express himself in the language of the common man and was liked as just another draftee in C Company. Yet, a worldly self-assurance was an innate part of his nature; he possessed a certain confidence that could not be suppressed.

The train rumbled into the distance, and Patrick's musings were brought back to reality. He had a meeting to attend and a daughter to pick up.

Chapter Four

Optimists are those rooted in the conviction that we should opt for the right way, the moral path, living out the good in life, and always being thankful to a gracious God. Pessimists give up on others, on themselves and, eventually, on life. Those who search for the lowest common denominator always find it, at a high cost to joy and peace in their lives. But to those who view life as a journey, even as a great adventure, and face the ebb and flow of life with conviction and courage, they are more than survivors. They are strong, intrepid spirits who trod the earth in boldness, choosing to live life standing erect, walking in the light. Only liars, cheaters, murderers need to slink in darkness, hiding their wickedness from sight.

• • •

Patrick sensed Joe's charisma from the first time he met him. He came from a prominent family, at least by Indiana standards, and bore his pedigree with the confidence that comes from wealth and station. He was a handsome man, taller than Patrick at six feet, two inches, with finely chiseled features, a strong jaw, and a muscular, tan body that accentuated his sun-bleached hair.

While so many went to Vietnam because of an unlucky draw or an inability to pay for college, Joe went for other reasons. He intended to serve his country honorably and with distinction, because someday that record would serve him well. Joe admired John F. Kennedy, often recalling the photo of him sitting in PT-109, the sun streaming on his sandy hair, every bit the golden boy. That's what Joe dreamed of — a great photo op like that.

The friendship between the two men had always been an easy one, unencumbered with jealousy or pettiness. They were close in ways men consider themselves to be close. They golfed together, competed in racquetball, had lunches, talked over beer after work. Patrick enjoyed cookouts with Joe and his wife, Ricki, and their two children. Before Emily's death, Joe and Ricki had come to Patrick's house, too, for some of Emily's Irish cooking.

With Joe's intelligence and facile charm, he was a natural leader and friend to the staff, writers and editors of the *Observer*, as he was with the men in Charlie Company. Under his guidance, the *Observer* was a flourishing newspaper; his corporate rise was assured, and now he was ahead in the race for senator.

Joe was out for the day, again. His senate campaign was taking large chunks of his time with press conferences, dinners, fairs, and enough black-tie events to satiate even the most blatant social climber. But he still called in periodically to check on the development of articles or court proceedings in criminal cases.

On this morning, Patrick arrived early for work, hoping to finish an article before starting on the Harris trial. The ironic twists of the Harris trial kept readers' tongues wagging with disgust and uncharitable pleasure. Carl Harris, a married man with a six-year-old daughter, was on trial for murdering his seventeen-year-old girlfriend who, as it came out at trial, was pregnant, but not with his child.

Patrick was pondering the newest turn of this trial — whose baby was it? — when the phone rang. It was Joe, checking in on the workday.

"Hi, Pat. Hey, what's the inside story on the Harris trial? Do they know who the father of that baby is?"

"The police are working on it, checking out the girl's friends and acquaintances, but nothing has come up yet."

"Whoever the father is, it gives him a motive for murder. Of course, Harris has a reason to be murderously jealous, too. Just keep me up-to-date on this."

"I'll do that, Joe. Since the dead girl can't talk, the real father may be difficult to locate. Hey, do you think you could carve out a half hour in your busy schedule to talk with me?"

"Sure. What about?"

"Just some things I'd like to discuss." Patrick brushed off any sense of urgency; he didn't want to sound alarming. "How about tomorrow sometime?"

"Okay, I'm sure I can work it in. I'll talk to my campaign manager."

• • •

The 4 p.m. meeting was at Nigel's Pub, an upscale bar

and eatery in the heart of downtown Fort Summit. Patrick arrived first, and asked for a quiet table in an enclosed area where the two could talk undisturbed. Joe entered the Pub a bit late, but radiated confidence; the polls showed him up by five points against his opponent. Because of his visibility and ubiquitous face on posters and TV ads, some at the bar wanted to chum with a celebrity, discuss politics or ask for an autograph. Acknowledging them with a quick sweep of his hand, he headed to where Patrick was seated.

"What can I get you, Pat?" he said as the waiter arrived.

"I'll take a Guinness," Patrick said.

"Make it two."

"Steve told me the polls are really smoking for you," Patrick said.

"Yeah. Tomorrow I canvas the southern part of the state. I just have a few loose ends to tie up."

Leaning closer to Pat, Joe whispered, "You know, Pat, I have every intention of making you the executive editor for the paper when I'm in Washington. You have all of the qualifications that I'm looking for."

"I appreciate your confidence, Joe. I'd love the challenge."

Patrick shifted his eyes downward, mentally parsing his words about approaching the subject of Vietnam. "Uh, Joe, there is something that I need to discuss with you."

"That sounds ominous."

"It's about Vietnam, October 1969."

Joe's eyes bored into Patrick's.

"Do you remember?" Patrick asked.

"I couldn't forget. I doubt any of us have had a minute's peace since."

"Tom Becker told me about it, but he is concerned about what happened to the girl. And who may have killed her."

"Do you really think one of us would kill the girl, that we could do something like that?" Joe asked. "Pat, how long have we known each other? Look, we made a mistake, a big one, but murder? No, that couldn't happen."

"Tom said the girl's body was found the next day."

"That doesn't necessarily implicate any of us in C Company."

"No, but he said you dealt the cards; he also said that whoever got the ace of spades had to take care of the girl."

"I know I didn't use those words, but, yeah, maybe threaten her or scare her into silence. But, I assure you, nothing was said or even implied about killing her."

When the beer was served, Joe took a long drink from the mug. An awkward pause allowed one of Joe's staffers to break in with the latest stats.

"We're blowing their doors off," Bill exclaimed to Joe, a glass of wine in hand. Joe's smile was electric; he was on his way. When Bill left, Patrick was insistent on bringing the conversation back to its source.

"Tom said an order was given to disperse, then return to camp without anyone else knowing. Do you remember who gave that order?"

"Uh, I think it was Ralph. No, wait, it was Larry. He's the one. You know Larry, always had to be in charge. 'You can talk to my lawyer,' he would threaten."

"What happened after that?"

"I went back to camp and pretended to fall asleep. I admit it, I couldn't sleep, but I've tried to forget about it and live a good life."

"Is there anything else you can tell me, something somebody said or did that was out of the ordinary?"

"Nothing comes to mind. We were young, we were stupid, we did something that we are ashamed about. I'm sure the other guys regret it, too."

Patrick looked at Joe, his buddy in war, his friend, his employer. His eyes met the cold Guinness atop the barked wood on the table. "I hope you understand; I promised Tom I would find out what happened."

"I hope you do find out. Knowing you, you will. But I swear, I don't know what happened to that girl after we left her. I just know that I caused her no harm."

• • •

It only took a couple of calls to Army acquaintances for Patrick to find out where Ralph Sherman lived. He had moved to New Jersey, completed a master's degree in business management and founded a charitable organization: a football camp for underprivileged boys.

This fits perfectly with Ralph's philanthropic nature,

44

Patrick thought. He always expressed a desire to help people; he was driven by relationships and the emotional quality of life, never by money or status or power.

When the phone rang, Ralph had just finished eating and was about to play touch football with his younger son, 10-year-old Eric.

"Hello?"

"Ralph, this is Patrick O'Riordan, Charlie Company. I guess I'm a blast from the past."

"Pat! Hey, buddy! How the heck have you been?"

"Can't complain. What have you been up to?"

The conversation was lighthearted — Ralph had married and become the father of two sons. His income from the football camp was adequate, but his wife's recent employment as an accountant added to the family's coffers. Patrick briefly replayed the story of his wife's death, his daughter, his job at the paper, and, of course, Joe's management style and his senate run.

"I always knew Joe would make good as a newspaperman, even if his father did own the company," Ralph said. "He's a natural leader and knows how to get people on his team."

Patrick readily agreed with that assessment. His working relationship with Joe Randolph over the years had been a warm one, built on trust and friendship.

"I do have a problem, though, and I need to talk to you about it."

"It sounds so serious. What's going on?"

"Last week, I spoke with Tom Becker. He has terminal cancer, maybe has only three months left." Patrick heard a compassionate groan from Ralph, then continued. "This is a difficult subject to broach, so I may as well step right in. Tom asked me to investigate something for him, something that happened in Vietnam, an incident he wants resolved, and he asked me for help to get to the bottom of it."

The silence at the other end of the line was telling. "Ralph, are you still there?"

The voice responded, but this time it was lower, softer. "Let me get on the phone in the bedroom; I can talk to you there." He picked up the phone next to the bed stand and told his son to hang up the first receiver, then waited for the click to make sure he had obeyed.

"I know what incident Tom is referring to — the young girl," he stammered.

"Yeah. Can you tell me about it?" Patrick asked.

"I remember starting out with some of the guys that night — Tom, Larry, Joe. Rick went along, too. We were looking for Vietcong and loaded for bear."

He drew a deep breath, then added, "Do you remember how much I used to drink back then? I really had a problem, although I couldn't admit it for a few years. On that night, I polished off a six-pack and was working my way down a bottle of Jack Daniels. I was already smashed by the time we went on patrol.

"I remember coming across the couple. The boy took off; the girl, well, she was shaking, terrified. I don't

46

know who first unzipped," he paused. "I think it was Rick, but — . "It may have been Tom who went second. I can't tell you how many times I've asked for forgiveness, and I still can't forgive myself."

"I need to talk to you about it," Patrick said. "Tom said the girl was murdered."

Ralph took a long, deep breath, then said, "I think it was Larry who first suggested doing something about silencing her, although I can't even be sure of that. As I said, I was pretty drunk. Then Joe pulled out a deck of cards. He started dealing them. He said whoever gets the ace of spades will have to take care of the problem."

"Then what happened?"

The silence on the line evinced deep anguish.

"I couldn't do it — even as drunk as I was. Yes, I got the ace, but I couldn't kill her. I checked on the girl; she was hurt pretty bad, but she was alive. I waited for a minute or two, trying to clear my head. I felt her pulse, cut the ropes on her wrist and staggered back to camp."

Ralph's desperation was evident with his panicked whisper. "I didn't know what to do! We all agreed not to tell anyone, *anyone*. We left separately, and when I got back, I drank even more. I wanted to convince myself that it was all a bad dream. Remember Pete, Pete Fogel? We were drinking buddies back then."

"Yes, I remember Pete."

"I told him. I know I wasn't supposed to, but I ..." Ralph's voice trailed off, then he said, "I was so smashed, I passed out and fell asleep on the floor of the latrine until Larry woke me up. I *know* I didn't kill her, but I have no idea who could have."

"When you came back, do you remember who arrived at base last?"

"I don't know. I grabbed my bottle and didn't stop. I didn't see any of the others that night."

"Any idea how I could reach Pete Fogel?"

"No, no idea."

"Did you hear anything, see anything, that might have led you to suspect someone?"

"No," Ralph said. "As I said before, I was smashed out of my mind, and we were all guilty. We knew it."

• • •

A newsroom is a busy place. In many ways, it reminded Patrick of a beehive. The newspaper is the queen. To be fed, she sends out workers to gather news for her and disseminates it into royal jelly and honey, sustaining both the queen and her workers. The constant clacking of typewriters, with the daily comings and goings of reporters and writers, are the hum of life in the hive. It is the epicenter of information: Whatever is happening in this city, or around the world, the newsroom is the hub.

• • •

(The last day of Patrick's life)

Patrick's hours were long on that fateful July day; he came in earlier than usual and left late. His parents stayed the night before, then took Katie to their lake cottage that morning to spend a few days, as she often

48

did during the summer. His daughter loved the lake just as he did as a child, and now that his parents had bought the cottage of his grandparents, the memories were even more treasured. He could relive his happy youth through the dancing eyes and melodic laughter of his cherished daughter.

Patrick noticed the sun was setting when he got in his car, its warm, golden rays dappling through the trees and buildings. He had one more thing he had to do before sleeping: he had to drive to Sycamore, taking State Road 3. A man named "Bud" had information about the Harris trial that he said might prove "interesting" to the case. After that, he would grab a good book and settle in for the night. He had no premonition how long the sleep would be.

Chapter Five
Several Years Later

Kate O'Riordan stood mesmerized at the large framed photo of her father, dramatically hung in the entryway of *The Fort Observer*. Even though she saw it every work day, her father's honest face and wise, knowing eyes held deep meaning for her. It affirmed her father's presence, at least in her heart. But today was even more special: It was Patrick's birthday, a day that she and her grandparents observed each year.

Although she had loving grandparents who reared her, her heart often ached for her father, even now. She cherished such vivid memories — his enthusiastic laugh, his wit, his depth of character, his nurturing kindness. Patrick tried to live life large, not in outrageous actions or narcissistic bravado, but with a generous dollop of optimism that could not, would not be dispelled, despite the buffets of life.

His daughter stood 5'8" tall, with her parents' trim figure and hair the color of strawberry blonde. His spirited temperament and deep sense of duty lived on in her, too, and she held her father even closer for it. She even liked her coffee the way her father did — the creamy tan color of supple leather. I am my father's daughter, she thought.

Her reverie was broken by the voice of fellow reporter Randy Thompson.

"Kate, have you finished the Ogden story?"

"I'm going to wrap it up today."

"Good. I just found out the prosecutor accepted a plea-bargain for manslaughter."

"Thanks for the heads up. I was going to call, but you saved me the trouble."

Although Randy had worked for the paper only about five years longer than Kate, he liked to think of himself as Kate's mentor, at least in a helpful, big-brother way. Kate appreciated his concern, yet sometimes wanted to say, "Hey, I can take it from here." But especially on this day, however, she held her tongue and cherished the remembrances of her father.

● ● ●

Newspaper people can be a fickle lot. They'll work at a small paper for just long enough to launch them to an even larger paper or publication. Because *The Fort Observer*, and Fort Summit, were mid-size markets, the exit gate was usually as busy as the entry one.

There were three people, however, who worked during the years that Kate's father did and were still employed by the paper: Lucille Roth, Mary Bleeke and Sam Owen.

Lucille started out as a features writer who was promoted to department editor four years ago. Mary was responsible for obituaries, weddings, engagements and "soft" news briefs for, well, as long as anyone could remember.

Sam was now managing editor, an invaluable asset to

the executive editor, Doug Richmond, who was not "home grown." Sam knew the market, the people, the city perhaps better than anyone else at the paper.

He could sometimes seem aloof, even hardened, on the surface. Yet inside, he had a passion for what he did: inform people with the complete story, give the pros and cons, then let them decide for themselves. He had an innate respect for people and believed that if they had complete information they would usually arrive at the best decision.

From the first time he heard of Patrick's death, Sam had a disquieting feeling that it was not merely an accident. He kept his misgivings to himself, but he often wondered if he shouldn't have expressed his doubts to Patrick's parents. Seeing Kate now, he felt a strong urge to say something to her.

• • •

The envelope was placed next to her keyboard, where Kate was certain not to miss it. Its faded, torn corners and frayed edges manifested its age. There was no name or identification; it was merely an old 9" x 12" envelope stuffed with pages of notes, names, phone numbers, etc. But Kate's heart almost stopped when she looked at the bold handwriting: It was her father's! Someone had placed her father's notes on her desk. She glanced quickly around the room, trying to spot anyone who may be observing her, but everyone appeared to be absorbed in work, totally oblivious to her discovery.

The pages were not in any semblance of order, but,

upon further scrutiny, it was apparent the hodgepodge of notes contained names and information that Patrick was investigating.

Let's see, she thought, there's a number for Tom Becker. I vaguely remember him. He died several years ago, I think. Ralph Sherman, Rick Schmidt, Larry Anders, Pete Fogel — I don't know any of them. But these dates in June 1983, right before Daddy …. It appears that he called them about something. Was it after or before he spoke with Tom? Perhaps this will explain where he was going that night, and why.

No one could explain why Patrick was on State Road 3 that ominous night. Upon his early arrival that morning, he had told several that he couldn't wait to go home and get lots of sleep. And when the accident occurred in a location that was in the opposite direction of Patrick's home, everyone wondered where he was headed. Even his parents' cottage, a straight northerly direction on I-69 from Fort Summit, wouldn't take him that far east.

Kate looked at the addresses by each name. Ralph lived in New Jersey — that's certainly east of here, she thought, Rick in Pass City — nope, that's southeast, Larry in Baker — could Dad have been headed for Ohio? She pulled out an atlas and scanned Ohio. Baker is tucked into the northwest corner of Ohio, a trip that could require taking State Road 3.

I wonder if that's where Dad was going. Perhaps some of these phone numbers are still correct, she thought, quickly dismissed the idea, then came back to it. Well, she reasoned, some people do live a long time in one house. It's possible. I would at least like to find the connection between these men, and discover what Dad was working on. It may shed some light on the accident.

"Kate, better hurry. You know how Doug hates people coming in late." The voice was Randy's, again, making sure Kate doesn't stumble on the job.

"Sure. Be right there." Kate placed the envelope behind her computer, out of sight. She wasn't sure why she wanted to hide these long-lost notes, she just knew this was one case she would work on herself, quietly. Then she quickly left for the meeting, displaying her father's penchant for promptness.

● ● ●

Sissy the cat was sleeping on the back of the couch, her favorite place, "ruling the world," as Kate put it, when Kate walked through the door. The black tabby was taking advantage of the sunny rays that filtered through the window. Sissy staked out her claim in Kate's small apartment and fashioned herself the real proprietor, merely allowing her roommate to hang her clothes there. When Kate found the kitten, or perhaps the kitten found her, she was a stray — cold, hungry and frightened. It was the last adjective that gave her the name "Sissy."

The kitty elevated her head toward Kate's gentle strokes and purred in agreement to her kind murmurings. "Did you guard the apartment well today, Miss Sissy? Did you have a tough day on the couch?"

It was always necessary for Kate to minister to her cat first when she came home. If not, Sissy would rub Kate's ankles and tap a paw on her legs, mewing lightly at first, then more insistently, if Kate did not respond in quick order.

After devouring a salad, Kate took the envelope with her father's notes and scattered its contents on the table. She decided to call Larry first for two reasons: he lived east of Indiana and, being from a smaller town, she surmised he may well be at the same address and phone number. The kitchen clock struck one bell; it was 6:30. Good, Kate thought, that would be 7:30 Ohio time. I won't be interrupting his dinner.

A woman answered with a sleepy "Hello."

"Hello. May I speak with Larry Anders, please?"

"Um, who is calling?"

"This is Kate O'Riordan. He doesn't know me, but I think he may have known my father, Patrick O'Riordan."

The muffled noises on the other line assured Kate that Larry was at home.

"Who is this, again?" This time the voice was clearly male.

"Kate O'Riordan, daughter of Patrick O'Riordan."

"Okay," Larry responded, "What can I do for you?"

"Mr. Anders, I happened to come across some notes that my father had written shortly before he, uh, his accident. There were several names written down, and I was hoping that you may be able to shed some light on this matter."

"What are the names?"

"Well, let's see, there's a Rick Schmidt, Tom Becker, Ralph Sherman, Pete Fogel, Joe Randolph and, of course, your name. Mr. Anders, is there any connection here?"

"Yeah, we were all in the same company in Vietnam." His voice sounded peevish.

"You were in Charlie Company with my dad? You and all the others?"

"That's what I said."

"Do you have any idea why my dad would have written your names down and contacted all of you?"

"No."

"Uh, Mr. Anders, I won't take much more of your time. On the night of the accident, my father was headed east on State Road 3. He lived on the west side, and my grandparents' cottage was north. Do you know why he might have been on that road, heading in the direction he was?"

"No," then he added, "I heard about the accident a week after it happened. Rick called me; he said he saw the death notice in the paper. He said Patrick died in a car accident. I don't know anything else about it."

"Do you have a recent phone number for any of these men?"

"Tom died several years ago. I haven't spoken to the rest of 'em in years."

"I appreciate your time, Mr. Anders. If you think of anything, anything at all, that may shed some light on this matter, please call me."

After leaving her number, she thanked him again and hung up.

• • •

Kate acknowledged the fact that Larry was probably telling the truth about Tom's death. She vaguely remembered her father saying something about Tom's cancer and how saddened he was to lose a friend. Yet she wasn't convinced that Larry was being completely honest with her, and she knew she wasn't going to stop her quest.

With access to Internet information, she would probably be able to locate these men within a day, if they were still alive. Of course, there was always "uncle" Joe. Now in his third term as senator, he had remained a steadfast family friend, never forgetting to send Kate gifts for her birthday and Christmas. His notes of encouragement were more frequent at first, shortly after Patrick's death, and his occasional monetary support, especially during Kate's college years, was deeply appreciated.

Joe would help her with information, Kate was certain, but she decided to contact him only as a last resort. He was a busy man, and a powerful one, and she didn't intend to clutter his schedule with her tenacious curiosity.

• • •

It has been said that we have many acquaintances in this life, but fewer friends, real friends. If that is so, then among Kate's real friends, Tri Nguyen was one of the best.

Tri (pronounced Tree) hailed from Vietnam but came to America a couple of years after U.S. troops pulled out in 1975. He first fled into southern Laos with his mother, who was in the dying stages of pneumonia, then entered Thailand. His father was a casualty of war. Only by sheer force of will did Tri survive.

Eventually, he was brought to America through the kindness of a local church organization that had helped thousands of displaced people after South Vietnam fell. When he arrived in Fort Summit, he was greeted at the airport by a welcoming committee, which had provided him with an apartment, some clothes, even a job.

He attended night classes at Indiana University's Fort Summit campus and majored in journalism. He still chuckles at the irony. He barely spoke any English when he first arrived, though he was familiar with some of the saltier expressions he'd heard used by American troops, and now he was a writer.

Tri had a steely resolve that would not be broken. He would not just survive in this bustling new country, he resolved, he would thrive. Journalism was one of the best ways for Tri to learn this puzzling English language.

It took him 10 years to graduate, but Tri relished in the euphoria that filled his heart. Grasping his diploma so tightly he almost left permanent indents, he knew he would always remember that day.

Even though he was approaching forty, he never

married, never fathered children, never participated in the social fabric of the city. He was a reporter for *The Fort Observer*, and that was the sum of his life, and he possessed a quiet strength and wisdom borne of tribulation. Kate knew, whenever she needed sound advice concerning her livelihood, Tri's counsel was always dead on.

• • •

Kate's alarm jangled stridently. Looking at the time, she realized that she had forgotten to set the clock earlier. Her feet quickly hit the cold floor as she chided herself for oversleeping on this morning, when she had an early meeting with the executive editor and the metro staff. She arrived at the stroke of seven, poured a steaming cup of coffee, added cream and quickly found her seat.

The paper was considering a "retro" series about Vietnam, then and now. Tri would be the paper's biggest asset and the chief writer for the series, and Sam Owen, the paper's veteran during those years, would lend insight into stateside stories about families, personal testaments, and the culture of the '60s and early '70s.

Kate begged to work with Tri, pleading her case as the daughter of a soldier who served in Vietnam. Tri agreed that Kate would be a great asset who would lend a younger, uncorrupted eye on those turbulent times. And Kate also knew that this opportunity would be her best entrée into solving her own small puzzle about

Vietnam: those five names and the connection they had with her father.

After the early edition was out, there was time to discuss the first account in the series with Tri.

"I think I'll start with a brief narrative about the French occupation, the struggle for independence from the Communists, then bring the readers to 1962, when President Kennedy ordered consultants to Vietnam, not just war materiel, as Truman and Eisenhower did," Tri said. "This first installment is key to understanding everything else."

"Especially since a large portion of America did not live through those years," Kate said, "and are as uninformed as I am about them."

Tri smiled in agreement, then Kate added, "Perhaps none of this will be helpful to you, but I would like to shed some light on these men."

She pulled some papers out of the envelope and showed Tri her father's notes. "Evidently, my father served with them in Vietnam, and he apparently had called them or was going to call them, but for what reason, I don't know. I was able to reach this guy — Larry Anders — but he wasn't forthcoming with information. And this person — Tom Becker — has passed on."

Tri's curiosity was piqued. "Where did you find these notes?"

"Someone laid them on my desk, where I would be certain to find them, but I don't know who."

"Write down these names for me, and their former numbers, and I'll see what I can find out."

• • •

As usual, Tri was still working in the newsroom when most of the paper's staff left to go home to family and friends. He filled these lonely evening hours with the love of his life — his work. His diligence did not go unnoticed. He had offers from larger papers, was seduced with higher pay, bigger titles, better perquisites, but Tri stayed at the "Fort." He was happy in his adopted city, he said, this is where he belongs, and that was as much explanation as he would give.

Searching for the names on the Internet, Tri mused about having the world's information at his fingertips, something he could never have imagined as a boy. Even if he had grown up in America, he couldn't have foretold such a worldwide wealth of knowledge at the stroke of a key.

That's it, he thought, Schmidt, Rick. Scanning 15 people with that name, Tri found the right one: "Corporal, U.S. Army, Vietnam, 1968-71, b. 1948, Pass City, Ind." Schmidt's current address and phone number were listed in Indianapolis, Ind. The others were found almost as easily. Larry Anders was still on the farm. Ralph Sherman was at a different address but lived in the same city. Pete Fogel was the toughest to locate. After Vietnam, he showed up in several locations but never stayed for very long. Tri's eyebrows shot up when he read the next lines. "Kansas City, Kan., jailed six months, assault & battery, 1975; Pendleton Prison, Pendleton, Ind., two years, drug dealing, 1978-80; arrested, Meadville, Pa., DUI, charges dropped, 1989." There were several other arrests, though no more convictions, yet Pete appeared to be living life on the fringe. The last address on record was in Plainfield, N.J.

I know where to start, Tri thought. We'll see if Mr. Fogel is very forthcoming.

Chapter Six

"The 'chief' liked the first article," Tri said, using an understood term for the paper's executive editor, Doug Richmond. "He says the background we gave on Vietnam's history will be a good segue into the rest of the series."

"I think we'll all be learning a lot more about Vietnam," Kate added.

"Perhaps more than we ever bargained for." His voice bore a tinge of wistfulness. "By the way, I located those names you gave me. Ralph Sherman is still in New Jersey, at this address; Rick Schmidt is in Indy," he said, handing her a slip. "But this guy Pete Fogel has a record. Just minor stuff mostly, although he did two year's time for dealing."

"Hmm. I think I'll give him a call."

• • •

Pete Fogel started chain smoking shortly after he arrived at his apartment, a compact, upstairs flat in a 1920s shingled house reconverted into separate living quarters sometime around the '60s. The blinking light on the answering machine was rarely a good omen. *Why did he let that slick salesman talk him into it?* Men like Pete had lost touch with family, friends and cheerful messages a long time ago.

He reluctantly pressed the message button.

"Mr. Fogel, my name is Kate O'Riordan, and I am a

reporter at *The Fort Observer* newspaper in Fort Summit, Ind. My father was Patrick O'Riordan. I understand you served in Vietnam with my father's company. I would appreciate talking with you. I won't take much of your time. Please call me at —"

His clothes, always soiled from his job in the quarry, matched the dingy interior of his lodgings. He was, again, officially "on the wagon" after a close brush with the law when he left his local bar with too much whiskey in his gut. He figured he could make the short drive home; he'd only had a few belts. But when he stumbled into his car, fumbling to put the key into the ignition, he saw the officer approach him.

"I wouldn't try it, buddy. You start that car, you're busted. Better call a cab."

Pete was convinced a DUI would land him in prison, and that thought was a big persuader to stop drinking. One thing at a time, Pete reasoned, first the booze, then the smokes. And then this message. Would he never be able to escape the memory of what happened in that god-forsaken land?

He lit another cigarette, failing to notice the smoke still encircling the first one, and picked up the phone. He memorized the number long ago, even though he'd only dialed it twice in the last 10 years. He delivered a terse message on the answering machine: "We need to talk," gave his phone number and brusquely hung up.

He took a deep pull on his cigarette, forcing smoke through his nose and clenched teeth. I need to have a plan, he consoled himself. I think I'll write everything down, then if something happens …

Although in all of his dreary, wayward existence Pete could rarely remember being happy, life was still something he grasped on to white-knuckled, with an instinctual desire to live.

Charlie Company provided the closest facsimile to family, yet Pete's story was standard fare for the skids of society. Father abandoned the family when Pete was a baby. His mother's life was a trash heap of unfulfilled dreams and a dead-end job cleaning hotel rooms. At the end of a day, worn out, sick and depressed, she often took to her bed, expecting Pete's older sister, Sally, to care for him.

At the time, Pete didn't appreciate the burnt hot dogs or the crusty macaroni and cheese Sally prepared. He yearned for meal times with a family, a real family, eating together, laughing, talking. But now he understood how hard his sister tried to bring a semblance of normality to their bleak situation.

He hadn't talked to her in a couple of years but not because she didn't keep trying. Sally married an electrician, reared three children and led a quiet, law-abiding life in southern Indiana. The last message she left for Pete merely said, "Pete, this is Sally. Please call me sometime. I'd like to talk. I hope you're doing well."

He wasn't certain what prevented him from calling her. Perhaps, he reasoned, it was the debris of his subsistence that he didn't want to explain. What could he say, other than his life was at least as barren as his mother's. He was embarrassed, and he knew it. Sally had more than survived; she had made a good life for herself and her family — she had friends, a comfortable home, the respect of those who knew her. He had a record, a washout job, a brief marriage that ended in divorce, no close family or friends, and a boatload of shame.

• • •

Ralph Sherman's wife, Denise, picked up the phone just as her granddaughter, Samantha, spilled more cake batter on the countertop than she got in the pan.

"Hello?" she said, "Oh, sweetie, we'll get that up. Sit the bowl here, and I'll help you in a minute." Then she said, "Hello?" again.

Kate, momentarily flustered, hesitated until the second hello kicked in her response.

"Uh, Mrs. Sherman, my name is Kate O'Riordan. I'm the daughter of Patrick O'Riordan, whom, I believe, served in Charlie Company with your husband."

"Yes, yes, I do remember that name. I think Ralph said your father passed away some years ago."

"Yes, that's correct. I would like to speak to your husband, if he is available."

"He's outside playing football with our grandson. Just a moment; I'll get him."

Ralph's voice was kind, but he spoke in whispered tones. The authoritative voice softly said, "Kate, how are you doing? Your father was a fine man; I was so

68

sorry to hear of his passing. What can I do for you?"

"I'm doing well, thank you. I just have a couple of questions, mostly out of curiosity, that I'd like to ask you."

"Okay."

"I came across some of my father's notes just before his — accident, and they contain the names and phone numbers of several men in Charlie Company. Was he planning a reunion or was there another reason for contacting you?"

Ralph took a deep breath, his sigh emanating across the wires, then said quietly, "No, he wasn't planning a reunion." There was another pause, another deep sigh, then the quiet voice again. "Kate, is there any way you could come here so we could talk? I will explain why your father called, but I can't do it on the phone."

Kate was perplexed, then frightened, by the serious tone this conversation had taken.

"Well, perhaps I could take a few days off. I could make the trip by car in a day. I also called Pete Fogel, and he lives in New Jersey in, uh, Plainfield. I'd like to talk to him, too."

"Pete called me about a month ago. He's had a tough life, been to prison, in and out of jail. But this time, I could sense a growing maturity in him. He said he wanted to start fresh, change his life. I really think he was sincere. He joined a church, said he was gonna call his sister and mend fences. When you come out here, we can talk to him together."

Chapter Seven

Tri's interest displayed more than a reporter's curiosity when Kate informed him about her call with Ralph. She wanted to take a few days off, she said, to talk to Ralph, and Pete, face to face.

"I think we could incorporate their accounts into the series we're doing," Tri said. "Every soldier has a story to tell."

Kate's eyes clouded over, then she said, "I think there's more than just a soldier's story here. Mr. Sherman did not want to talk to me over the phone, and Mr. Fogel has not returned my call. It's been a week since I phoned him." She gazed at the floor, piecing her words together with care. "Something — happened, something terrible, I can feel it. Perhaps my father was on the verge of discovering it, or maybe — maybe he was part of it. I don't know. But they all seem to be hiding something."

Something terrible, Tri thought. That's one way to describe the atrocities with which he was well acquainted. What he saw as a young man in Vietnam made him old long before his body caught up. His eyes were piercing when he asked, "What makes you think that?"

"Mr. Sherman made certain he couldn't be heard when he took my call, and even then, he wouldn't discuss anything. And just the way his voice changed when I brought up the subject of my father and the purpose of his call. Something happened, Tri, I know it."

Tri knew he was overstepping his boundaries, but he made an impulsive decision to have Kate go on this interview.

"I can talk to Doug. I'm sure he can have the paper pay for your mileage and room for a few nights," he said. "This is a story worth pursuing. When you get there, stay in close touch. Call me often; inform me of everything you can. Take your tape recorder, too. And please be careful. Terrible secrets have a way of turning into grave consequences."

• • •

Be careful. Terrible secrets. Grave consequences. Kate mulled the words to herself in rhythmic motion to the swish, swish of her windshield wipers. Her mood was reflected in the gray, dingy March skies overhead and the watery gloom that soaked her car and mopped the slippery road ahead. Was it raining when Dad …? She couldn't finish the thought, at least not the words, but a dark feeling remained, as if she were entering a malevolent realm of lies, deceit, danger. Was this scene played out by her father?, she wondered. Is it possible he was on the verge of discovering something that was hushed up so long ago?

She flipped on the radio just to get her mind off this obsessive merry-go-round. Dwelling on speculations and conjecture accomplishes nothing, she reminded herself. Instead, she would clear her thoughts of unsubstantiated suspicion, and meet Mr. Sherman with a welcoming hand and an open mind.

It was nearly 7 p.m. when she arrived at the two-story colonial home, with its well-maintained tidy exterior. She rang the doorbell and felt her stomach lurch at the thought of her mission.

An attractive, 50-something woman opened the door dressed in a long-sleeved white silk blouse and green slacks that accentuated her trim figure. Her formerly black hair was salt-and-pepper, and her dark eyes radiated a gentle nature that Kate recognized in her grandmother.

"Mrs. Sherman?" The woman's pleasant smile gave assurance of that. "I'm Kate O'Riordan, daughter of Patrick O'Riordan. My father and your husband served together in Vietnam."

"Yes, Kate, my husband told me. Please come in and sit down. I'll get Ralph."

Kate was directed into the living room, a compact but tastefully decorated area with a bay window that allowed a glimpse of the green expanse of neighbors' yards with children at play.

A large, muscular man entered the room with a two-barreled handshake that could have rattled the windows. Although his hair was completely gray, the broad smile that crinkled the eyes betrayed his identity. Kate had seen the photos of Charlie Company, and she recognized this older version of Ralph.

"You must be Kate," he said. "Let me look at you. You

73

were certainly the apple of your father's eye. When your mother died, we were all worried about him. I know it was a terrible time for him, but, as he told me, 'I have a child, Ralph, I have to keep going for her.' And that's what he did. He took it one day at a time."

Cradling Kate's hands in his, he gazed into her face. "Ah, yes, I can see your father's eyes," he said, "and your mother's radiant smile."

"I have been told I have my father's eyes, and his bulldog nose for news." Kate's eyes peered into Ralph's face as her voice became lower and softer. "Mr. Sherman, I have stumbled onto something that, well, I must get to the bottom of.

"My father was working on a story right before, uh," she cleared her throat, "that apparently concerned his Army buddies in Vietnam. He wrote down several names, yours among them, with phone numbers and cursory information about an event sometime in the fall of 1969. Any insight or information you could give me would be greatly appreciated."

Denise Sherman was just bringing in coffee for everyone when she noticed an uncomfortable awkwardness in the room. Recovering quickly, she said, "I'll leave the pot and cups here, and you can serve yourselves."

"It's all right, dear," Ralph said. "Please, sit down." Ralph leaned over in his chair, placed two sturdy elbows on his knees and clasped both hands together. "I don't talk much about Vietnam; Denise can attest to that.

War is a terrible thing, but a war that was executed in such a purposeless way as this one was is even more destructive. We would be ordered to capture a hill, and we would do it, at the cost of human lives, our buddies' lives. Then we'd leave the area and allow the Vietcong to take it again. I mean, what was the point? I don't know if anyone had a clear understanding of why we were there, and what we were supposed to be doing while we were there.

"The atrocities we saw — even some of the children were our enemies. We felt we couldn't trust anyone. We were young, impressionable, and God knows we loved our country. But we were devastated by how the war was managed, the unflattering portrayals of soldiers and Vietnam vets by the American press, and especially by the mean-spiritedness of so many of our fellow countrymen. We felt betrayed by the people we thought we were defending, betrayed by our leaders, betrayed by our country.

"And we were angry. No," he corrected himself, "we were enraged. We were on the front lines, we didn't know if we were going to live or die, come home in a body bag or so damaged we couldn't walk, or ever see or hug our children again. And even if we were lucky enough to survive and come home in one piece, we were spat on, screamed at, vilified, described as baby killers or damaged goods.

"And those who didn't go, well, their smug arrogance was intolerable. Right after I got back, I got in a bar fight with an overbearing peacenik that I would've killed if my friends hadn't pulled me off of him."

Denise poured the strong, black liquid into mugs that steamed with its contents.

"Cream?"

"Yes, thank you," Kate said.

"In the fall of '69," Ralph began, "October 23rd, a date I'll never forget, our company was near Vinh Long. We'd been getting some sniper fire and someone told us the Vietcong were hiding out nearby. So, one night a few of us decided to go on a fishing expedition. We were gonna find these bastards and take 'em out.

"Your father didn't go. He'd stepped on something the day before, and his foot was red and swollen. Capt. Peterson was gone and left Steve Westoff in charge for the night. Pete Fogel was just getting over a bad bout of dysentery. There were only five of us, all fired up to do something. Rick Schmidt, Tom Becker, Joe Randolph, Larry Anders and I left in the dead of night and headed toward the area. As I said before, we were mad as hell.

"We didn't get there. Instead, we came across a couple, a young girl and her lover, in the woods. When the boy saw us glaring over both of them, he took off running, trying to pull his pants on at the same time. The girl was frozen with fear, her eyes pleading for mercy."

Ralph buried his eyes in his massive hands, regained his composure and continued, "I'm not making excuses for anything that happened or for anyone involved in what happened; I just want to explain what was going

76

on in our heads at the time. I was pretty soused, even before I set out, mixing beer and whiskey with abandon, just tryin' to dull the pain, I guess. Someone started in on the girl, maybe it was Rick, but I honestly don't remember. We all had our way with her; she was hurt and scared, but alive.

"Somebody tied her wrists to a tree. Then someone else said that we had to get rid of her. If she talked, we'd all be court-martialed. Joe always had a deck of cards — he loved playing euchre. Whoever gets the ace of spades will have to take care of the problem, he said. I guess we all knew what he meant; I just hoped I wouldn't have to face it. After the cards were dealt, we scattered, assuming that whoever got that detestable card would be stuck with what to do.

"I looked at my card in the moonlight and knew my worst fear had happened: I held the ace in my hands. I was a soldier who had killed Vietcong, who had seen his buddies wounded and dying, who faced death on a daily basis, but I knew I couldn't hurt that young girl. She'd been hurt enough. I went back and checked her pulse. I cut the ropes so she could go. But she was still alive when I left her."

Ralph's voice trailed off, then he said animatedly, "Don't you see? I couldn't do it! I just couldn't do it! I walked back to camp, almost weaving from the alcohol, pulled out my hidden bottle of whiskey and downed it.

"Pete was my drinkin' bud, and we both were packing it away. I broke down crying, talking through the booze to Pete about what happened that night. He said nothing; he just listened. I passed out shortly after that. I woke up next to a toilet; Larry was shaking my shoulder and ordering me to get up.

"But I know one thing for certain: I did not kill that young girl. I don't even know for sure if she *was* murdered, but if she was, I have no idea who did it."

Ralph's eyes were dark hollow wells of sadness. The silence that encompassed the room was unbearably loud. Kate and Denise, who apparently had heard this tale for the first time, appeared visibly shaken.

"Then this, this incident, must be what my father was looking into," Kate said softly.

"Yes, he called, told me that Tom was dying and didn't want to go to his grave with this terrible secret on his soul. Tom denied killing the girl, too, so that leaves only three others."

"Do you think Pete would be capable of such an act?" Kate inquired. "Do you think any of the other three would be?"

"When Pete called me, he said he had a lot on his mind, and he alluded to that night, when we got drunk together. He wanted to talk, he said, but first he wanted to mend a few fences. I think he meant with his sister, but he also talked of spiritual matters. He said he needed to 'get right with God,' whatever he meant by that."

Kate embraced the warm mug in her fingers, contemplating what she should do or say next.

"I'd like to talk with Pete," she said. "I have a recent address. Could I talk you into going with me?"

A feeble smile washed across Ralph's weathered features. "I was hoping you'd ask," he said.

Chapter Eight

Pete sprawled on his compact bed, stewing about what the night might bring. In years past, when life seemed overwhelming, he would smoke or drink too much, or ingest an illegal substance, or all three, to ease the jumbled ball of pain that had governed his life. But tonight, after his tired old heart was reborn, he found deliverance in the Bible.

Romans 8 was the chapter Pete loved most because of its sweet assurances of certain victory. "There is therefore now no condemnation for those who are in Christ Jesus" moved him to the point of tears. Him, Pete, a man who had lived on the tattered edge of life from the beginning, who spit in God's face out of rage and bitterness, who hurt the people he loved most. "No condemnation;" how could this be? How could anyone love him so deeply? He couldn't even grasp this kind of love, yet he desperately wanted it, needed it, more than anything else.

"For I am convinced that neither death, nor life, nor angels, nor principalities, nor things present, nor things to come, nor powers, nor height, nor depth, nor any other created thing, shall be able to separate us from the love of God, which is in Christ Jesus our Lord."

The words seared his soul. All things are nothingness; God's love is everything.

He did not hear the dark figure that entered through

his unlocked door. Nor did he hear the sandpaper sound of a drawer sliding open, its metal handle gently rapping the wood.

The television below his apartment, the one that belonged to Mrs. Ashby, his landlady, was blaring with a din that would startle the deaf. Pete did notice, through the crack under his bedroom door, that the glow of a flashlight appeared to be in his small living room.

"Hello?" he said. When no one answered, he placed the Bible on his dresser and sat upright. Should he face this intruder? Should he fight for his life? What life? He began to pray as he saw the bedroom door inch open, just enough to allow the barrel of a gun, Pete's gun, to point directly at his head.

The crack of a single shot merged with the strafing pepper fire of an old war movie. Mrs. Ashby, asleep or passed out, was oblivious. Others in the neighborhood, with rare exception, were unable to see past their own small lives; they were usually too embroiled in their own dysfunctional existence. On this night, however, the neighbors noticed an impressive car, a well-dressed visitor and a cab.

The killer placed the gun in Pete's right hand, turned off the bedroom light, quietly shut the apartment door and descended the steps on tiptoe, his dark clothing concealed by the inky mantle of night.

• • •

The trip to Plainfield gave Kate some time to hear

Ralph relay old Army stories, humorous remembrances of a bleak time when Charlie Company tried to laugh its way through hell.

"I would never want to go through that time again," Ralph said, "but I thank God every day that I did." He took a swig from a water bottle, then added, "I realized the value of human life, how important family and friends are. And I learned how to depend on myself — and how to depend on others, too. Sometimes, we learn the most when the times are the worst."

"I'm glad I got to know a little more about my father," Kate said. "I knew him as a father, but listening to you gives me a different perspective."

"Your father was one of the finest men I've ever known," Ralph added. "He was a man of principles and morals with abundant courage, lots of smarts and a quick sense of humor. He was respected by everyone who knew him."

Kate blinked away the moisture that filled her eyes. She had spent so much time in her younger years obsessing on the unfairness of life, sometimes even shaking her fist at God, relentlessly beseeching Him with the one question that could not be answered: *why*.

Never in this world would she know the answer. Perhaps, in the next realm, with an elongated view of her life, of her father's life, of her mother's life, the answer may be made clearer. As for now, she realized that we see life events as a shaft of light; yet we gaze through a side window and miss the full frontal view.

We see the bright rays descending, dust motes suspended in the air, a portion of the room in a yellow bask of sunshine separated from the darkish exteriors surrounding it, but we cannot look directly into the light. The total picture is not ours to grasp. So much is hidden from us, from our understanding, from the answer to the one question that haunts us all: *why*.

"For now we see in a mirror dimly," St. Paul said.

"I'm also thankful I got to know you better, Ralph," Kate said. A warm smile eked its way across her face when she turned to him. "I hope we can solve this problem soon, with as little damage as possible to you or me or anyone else."

• • •

Ralph knew that Pete's life had been a hard one, but when the car pulled up to the dingy, gray-shingled house, he was struck by the tangible despair that permeated the air, sending a comfortless chill to the barren atmosphere. Even the sky mirrored the bleakness of the surroundings, or perhaps the other way around.

The exposed steps that ascended to Pete's apartment were weathered and bare. Kate and Ralph climbed them with trepidation, almost fearful of the man they may meet inside. Ralph knocked on Pete's door once, lightly, then again and again, his hand knocking more firmly with each attempt.

"No one is answering," Ralph said, then added, "Perhaps we should ask someone where he might be."

The landlady, who lived downstairs and rented the upstairs portion when her last child left home, was a small, wiry woman of undetermined age. Her teeth were in great need of repair, her blouse was soiled with food. A long swathe of thin gray hair was wrapped into a small bun that perched atop her head.

When asked about Pete, she said curtly, "I don't know where he is. I haven't seen him for two days. Usually I'll hear him going or coming to work, and he often goes to a bar over on Leech Street called Bucky's. You might check there."

"Does he have any family or friends we might call to ask if ..."

"No, no, he has nobody I know about, and he's lived here for five years."

"Where does he work?" Kate inquired.

"At the quarry," the woman stated flatly, "about half a mile down the road."

Ralph and Kate thanked the woman for her time, then asked one more question.

"If you haven't seen him in a couple of days, do you have a key to his apartment, so that we can check on him just to make sure he's okay?"

"Well, yeah, I do," she said hesitatingly, "but I'll have to go with you. I can't be giving out apartment keys to people I don't know."

"I understand," Ralph said, "and thank you."

The woman disappeared into her cluttered house, adorned with furniture from the '50s, cheap figurines of

85

cats and dogs, and a menagerie of trinkets, dolls and junk that centered around a huge color television set, probably no more than two years old.

She returned with a small key and a coat that she pulled on as the three ascended the steps. Knocking on the door several times, louder with each try, she gingerly moved the knob. The door, though closed, was unlocked. She peered her head in and looked around the small, dirty apartment.

"I told Pete many times he should take better care of this place," she said. Several dishes were in the sink, food crusted on them for days. A drinking glass, half full of soured milk, rested atop the lone television set, with full ashtrays everywhere, on tables, counters, even the toilet tank. The stink of stale cigarettes filled their nostrils, but another reeking smell was so foul, it almost caused their knees to buckle.

Ralph opened the bedroom door, then pulled his face away, grabbed a handkerchief and covered his nose. He knew that odor from Vietnam; it was the recognizable smell of death.

It was difficult to see in the blackened room with the curtains pulled together, so Ralph flipped the light switch, its harsh overhead bulb exposing a ghastly sight.

Pete was sprawled across the single bed, his mouth agape, with a small rivulet of dried blood from the corner of his mouth that encrusted itself on the threadbare sheets. He had been shot once in the head, its trajectory hitting in the lower middle forehead and out the back of the head, leaving a bloody seepage of bodily fluids and brain matter that gave an almost halo effect to the scene. His left arm bent upward below the shoulder, flayed open in frozen surprise. The fingers on his right hand were splayed around a gun. One blackened eye was open and seemed to peer at a wooden cross on the wall, the room's only adornment. A Bible was laying on the small dresser next to the bed, open to the book of Romans.

Kate turned her face and headed for the bathroom. She knew that whatever was left in her stomach would be coming up soon. Mrs. Ashby was distressed. How could this happen to her tenant right above her place? Was he murdered?

"I'll call the cops," she said as she scurried from the apartment. "I don't know how this could happen. What is the world coming to?"

Gathering his wits, Ralph made certain that he and Kate disturbed nothing more at the scene. They descended to the bottom of the stairs to wait until the police arrived, breathing deeply of the air that, previously, had seemed so stagnant, but now felt crisp and revitalizing.

"I'm sorry you had to see that, Kate," Ralph said. "Just keep taking deep breaths. Fill your lungs. How's your stomach?"

"Very queasy," Kate responded. "Do you think it was suicide or .... Why would someone want to kill him? *Why?*" she gasped. There it was again, the unanswerable question. So often she imagined herself the skeptic at the back of a crowded room, pumping her hand in the air and imploring of nature and nature's God — *why, but why?*

Chapter Nine

It was around 11 p.m. before Ralph and Kate were free to leave the police station. They had answered all the questions at least six times, it seemed, each time to a different investigator. And even though Kate responded truthfully and fully, she had several of her own unanswered questions.

The preliminary police investigation found that the gun was shot from a few feet away, and Pete had no gunpowder residue on his hands. It was definitely a murder.

• • •

Kate had made phone calls to Ralph, Larry, Rick and Pete; perhaps they had contacted each other. Perhaps they all had something to hide, and Pete was the renegade who would no longer remain silent. He may have made that clear to the others. Perhaps even Ralph was involved. Kate cringed as soon as this thought kicked its way to the fore of her mind. She liked Ralph; she liked him a lot. Even at her young age, she fashioned herself a good judge of people. Sometimes, of course, she was fooled, but she firmly believed her assessment of Ralph and his character were right on.

• • •

"I called Denise and told her we would be driving home tonight," Ralph said. "She was pretty shook up about what happened to Pete. She wonders if I'm next, if someone is trying to silence all of us."

"That thought crossed my mind, too," Kate said, keeping her other suspicions to herself. The two, almost numb with weariness, walked to the car in total silence, each absorbed in personal qualms and mistrust that enveloped their thoughts like a funeral sheath.

Ralph thumped his index finger on the steering wheel to the beat of '60s rock, playing softly on the car radio as a backdrop to an uncomfortable silence. But the music took him back to jungle heat and stench and blood and fear, to the putrid water of the Mekong Delta, to the fog of alcohol and the smell of death. And he recalled again that night, when the young girl's face registered such terrifying fear, the frightful look in her eyes through the moon's eerie glow, her short, shallow gulps of air to placate herself. He tried to forgive himself for what he did, and for what he did not do.

Did I in some way cause Pete's death, too? he wondered. *What am I missing?*

He went through the events again, the girl, the rape, the draw, the card. She was alive when I left her, he thought; he was certain of that. So why didn't she run? Was she physically too hurt? Emotionally too frozen? Ashamed? Afraid? *I should have moved her away from there,* he chided himself. Yet he knew why he didn't. She was like a baby bird, fallen out of its nest, too fragile to be picked up and placed back in the nest. He wanted only to leave, never think of this again, never see her face in his mind. But, of course, it was seared in his very being. He would remember it until his last breath.

Pete wasn't there (or was he?), but he knew about it. He knew because Ralph told him, even where the girl was left. Was he as drunk as I was? Could he have returned to that place, seen something, done something, that may have sealed his fate today?

• • •

As Ralph quickly changed channels to the symphonic sounds of classical music, Kate breached the silence with a pointed question.

"Is there anything you may have overlooked or forgotten that could have played a part in Pete's death?" she asked.

"You must be reading my mind," Ralph said. "I remember telling Pete about the incident, where the girl was when I left her, how I just couldn't kill her. I suppose he could've gone back after I passed out, maybe to check on her, but I can't believe Pete would just arbitrarily snuff her life. Yes, we were soldiers, and we killed, but — I just can't believe ..." His thoughts ran ahead while his voice trailed off.

"Was Pete involved in anything illegal, something that someone could hold over his head or threaten him with?" Kate asked.

"I know most people assume that all Vietnam vets were druggies, and some were, but I wasn't. And your father wasn't either," Ralph emphasized. "Although I had a problem with the bottle, well, some said that Pete was a dealer. Rumor had it that he'd buy drugs wholesale from someone in country, then distribute them to other soldiers. I swear I never saw him do that, but that was the buzz."

"Do you think that may have played a role in his death?"

"I suppose that's always a possibility. He was always in trouble, even in the service. Perhaps his past finally caught up with him, though I wonder why so many years have passed with no repercussions."

"I think we need to find out if Rick, Larry and Joe have been in touch with Pete," Kate said. "And if they know anything about the drug-dealing rumors."

"Yes, we do need to contact them, but will that put their lives in jeopardy, too?"

• • •

Kate called Tri as soon as she reached her motel room. Speaking in excited bursts of conversation, she informed Tri about what she had seen and heard.

"Tri, I got to Ralph's house, talked with him at length. He explained everything he could remember about that night in Vietnam. He said they found a girl with her boyfriend, and they raped her.

"Ralph was drunk that night, very drunk. After the assault, they drew cards, apparently with the understanding that whoever drew the ace of spades should handle the problem. Ralph drew the card, assuming he should kill her, but he couldn't do it, so he went back to camp and told his drinking buddy about the girl. That buddy was Pete Fogel.

"Oh Tri, it was awful! We drove to Pete's place, really shabby, and found his body. He's dead! Someone put a bullet through his head!"

Tri's shock displayed itself in his first stammering question.

"Wh-What? Pete was murdered? Do you have any idea why?" He knew, of course, the why could not be explained, at least not right now.

I'm doing it again, Tri admonished himself, I'm asking things I know can't be answered immediately.

Sometimes he would have a stream-of-consciousness reaction to shocking news or unexpected events, his thoughts racing ahead of his logic, causing his tongue to react in embarrassing and even foolish ways.

"We'll never know what he knew, or if he had any information," Kate said.

After a stunned silence, Tri said, "Get a good night's sleep. Come back to town tomorrow, and we'll talk then. Don't worry about this. Things will work out."

Kate hoped Tri's strength would be contagious. She got ready for bed and began to read her book — a Hercule Poirot mystery by Agatha Christie — to take her mind off recent events. She had to step back and think things through, she told herself, so she didn't miss something, some clue, some nuance, that might add light to this matter. She needed time to think, and she needed to rest so she could think.

Chapter Ten

During the long drive back, more questions raced through Kate's mind with each passing mile. Pete's death was murder, clear and simple. Her father's death was not clear and simple, but the thought pierced her mind. Was it an accident? Or was it murder?

When Kate met Tri the following day, the two discussed the investigation. In addition to the police dusting the apartment for fingerprints and searching for any foreign hair or body fluids, Tri called the investigators to check on phone records immediately. Who had Pete talked to recently?

"Ralph did say he talked to Pete about a month ago," Kate said.

"We can verify that," Tri said, then added, "I think I'll ask Ben Stuart about other clues to look for."

At twenty-seven, Ben was a rising star as deputy prosecutor for Wayne County. He had a good mind and a maturity of spirit that belied his youth. Although Kate had met him a handful of times, she felt an instant connection with him. He stood 6'1", with hair the color of dark chocolate and wide-set eyes that were as green as a shamrock.

His job required him to be a vigorous defender of the rule of law with an unbending desire to eradicate injustice. As a realist, he knew some victims were not entirely innocent, nor some perpetrators entirely bad, yet he approached his profession with an almost missionary zeal. His stridency, however, was put in check off the job. Although his serious demeanor was always professional at work, his ready smile and warm eyes betrayed a witty sense of humor and an undying spirit of adventure.

"I think talking to Ben would be helpful," Kate said. "We may miss something that he'll be able to see."

When Kate and Tri arrived at the deputy prosecutor's unimposing office, Ben was on the phone but waved them in and gestured for them to sit down. Surprisingly, the desk was uncluttered. Papers were neatly stacked in one pile, anchored with a clear glass paperweight bearing a picture of Abraham Lincoln; books, mostly law volumes, were methodically placed in library order.

A single photograph, displayed on the desk in a polished gold frame, showed a smiling baby girl resplendent in a red Christmas dress, whose dimpled, cherub features bore a slight resemblance to her uncle Ben.

A winter coat and an umbrella hung on a handsome coat tree, evidence of cold, sometimes wet Fort Summit winters, especially in March.

"Just let me know when the DNA evidence comes in," Ben said, "Okay. Stay in touch. Good-bye." Placing the phone back on its cradle, he said, "Kate, Tri, what can I do for you?"

Tri talked first, relaying the information found in Patrick's envelope, the troop that went out that night in

Vietnam, the young girl, the men whom Patrick contacted. Then Kate replayed her visit to New Jersey, her meeting with Ralph, and the horror of finding Pete's body.

Ben listened intently to Kate and Tri as they unfolded recent events, particularly the murder of Pete Fogel. Clasping his hands together, he placed his elbows on his desk and leaned toward his visitors, showing emotion only with a nod of his head or an upraised eyebrow.

"Look, Ben," Tri concluded, "I know this is not in your jurisdiction. Kate and I just want some direction about clues, procedures, evidence. Anything you could help us with would be greatly appreciated."

"I can do better than that," Ben smiled, "I know one of the prosecutors in that area. He was a law-school buddy, a good guy, Anthony Torrini. I'll give him a call, see if he can give us a heads-up on the investigation."

• • •

After she left Ben's office, Kate knew she needed to talk to an avuncular friend, someone who knew her parents, who has known her since she was a baby. Her beloved grandfather passed away two years ago; her "grammy" was in the middle stages of Alzheimer's. Though the clearness of her mind was muddled and confused, her sweet disposition emitted love and kindness from her caretakers.

Kate would visit as often as possible, delivering the dark, sweet chocolates her grandmother used to share

97

with Kate after the evening meal. Or sometimes she would buy a custard-filled doughnut topped with chocolate icing and watch her grandmother lick her fingers, enjoying its sticky delight. Grammy always had a weakness for sweets, a trait passed on to Kate.

Right now, she was missing all of them — her father, her grandparents, even her mother. As a child, she would gaze at her mother's picture, the one Patrick displayed next to his bed, and imagine her soft arms enveloping her, murmuring encouragement, the fresh smell of newly washed hair brushing her cheek. She never told her father of her fantasies, of course. He felt guilty and responsible enough as it was. And although no father could have been better, the thought of her mother would cause an ache in a place too deep to visit often.

She picked up the phone next to her bed stand and dialed the number, one she had remembered over the years. She was surprised and delighted that she didn't get the D.C. answering service.

"Ricki?"

"Yes." Her voice was formal and distant.

"This is Kate, Kate O'Riordan. How are you doing?"

"Kate!" The voice became ebullient. "It's so good to hear from you! We are doing well. And how about you?"

"Fine as well. I am so sorry I was unable to attend Susan's wedding, but I'm glad to hear everything was beautiful."

"You'll have to come out here to see the new home

Susan and Grant just purchased. It's in the Georgetown area, very close to where the Kennedys lived in the '50s." Jack and Jackie's charisma remains, Kate thought.

"I would love to do that," Kate said. "Perhaps in the fall I can get away."

After a little more small talk, Ricki said, "I'm sure you also want to talk to Joe. It's a rare happening, but he's home tonight."

"Kate," the familiar voice boomed, "how is everything in the Fort?"

"It's still interesting," Kate said, alluding to a statement she made to Joe several years ago when she confessed that she hoped her life would not be too tedious or dull.

"I'm glad to hear it. What can I do for you?"

"Joe, you know you've always been like an uncle to me, like family. And that's why I thought of calling you. Some really awful things have been happening, and I don't know where to go or who to turn to."

Joe's voice registered concern when he said, "Kate, what's wrong?"

"Do you remember Pete Fogel, the guy in Charlie Company with you and Dad?"

"Of course I do."

"Did you know that he was murdered?"

"No! How do you know this? I'm stunned. I don't understand. Why would anyone … "

"Did he call you recently, I mean, just shortly before he died?"

"Yes, he did, but he'd just leave messages on the answering machine. I admit, I never returned his calls. I haven't really talked to him in years. Kate, is everything all right? You didn't know Pete, did you? You seem to be taking this very personally."

"No, I didn't know him. I just wanted to talk to him about Vietnam and an article I'm working on. I went to see him, but it was too late. His death was so violent, it's shocking."

"Kate, I'm sorry."

"Could you fill in any more blanks — I mean, about his former wife, his sister, someone he may have stayed in touch with?"

"Mmm," Joe mused, "I don't know about his ex. He told me once his sister married; I don't know where she lives, though. Probably his best friend in the service was Ralph, Ralph Sherman. He might be able to answer your questions."

"Do you know where I could contact him?" Kate thought it best not to give out any information on the case.

"I heard awhile back he moved to New Jersey. I'd try there."

"Okay, thanks."

"I'll tell you what, you come out here, and I'll fill your ears with several stories about your father and me."

"I will, just as soon as I tie up a few loose ends here. I can't wait to see you both again."

Chapter Eleven

As Kate struggled to concentrate on an assigned article, a dry narration about local government's efforts to rezone downtown residential areas, she recalled the days when she dreamed of becoming a reporter, as she often did in her youth. The reverie replayed itself in her mind as an exciting quest, filled with adventure, fascinating cases, breaking news. Her expansive dream, however, did not include the day-to-day drudge work by young reporters on a beat, the stuff of which most reporting involves.

When her desk phone rang, she answered it with a languid "hello," then quickly found her interest reinvigorated when she recognized the voice on the other line.

"Kate? This is Ben. I got in touch with Anthony Torrini; he's working on the case and said he'd inform me of any new developments. Right now, they're checking phone logs. Apparently, Fogel did more long-distance calling the last three days of his life than he'd done for the last three years. Sounds like something was on his mind.

"Also, neighbors report that Fogel had two men visit him just two days before you found his body, one who pulled up in an expensive car, the other stepped out of a taxi. One man appeared well dressed, the other was dressed casually, common as dirt. No one was certain what kind of car the well-dressed man was driving; it was night, and the car was dark-colored, sleek and large.

"The guy who left the taxi was wearing a baseball cap, work boots, jeans, a jacket. One woman said she thinks he was white, but he also had gloves on, so it was hard to say because she didn't see his face.

"Two witnesses say the jeans guy in the cab arrived first, but one witness says he thinks the fancy car came first. Neither man stayed long, and they both arrived and left quietly."

"Mrs. Ashby told the police she hadn't seen or heard anyone for the last few days."

"Yeah, Torrini mentioned that. He said that Ashby keeps her TV on so loud at night she couldn't hear the Second Coming. And she's fond enough of gin martinis that she's usually passed out by seven. Both visitors came after that time.

"Any fingerprints found?"

"None but Fogel's and Mrs. Ashby's. Oh, and they found yours on the toilet tank, probably when you tossed your cookies."

A hot flush of embarrassment crossed Kate's face; she was glad she was on the phone. "I've always had a weak stomach," she said meekly, then regained her composure. "Well, let me know who Fogel called. I wouldn't be surprised if it's our little band of buddies."

• • •

Kate unlocked the door to her apartment and planted her purse on the side table. Ben had information about the phone records that she might find quite interesting, he said, so the two, with Tri, planned to meet at Jellicle's for coffee at seven-thirty. But before she could change into a comfortable pair of slacks and sweater, Sissy the cat demanded that her mistress render her attention. Bored after a long day of suncatching, Sissy insistently purred her approval as Kate rubbed behind her ears and stroked her back.

She decided to make a sketch of each suspect, where they were at, when they arrived and left, physical characteristics, personality, possible motive to kill, even gun ownership. It helped organize her thoughts, a concrete corroboration that linked the random, confusing clues of this case. She hoped it would lead to a "Poirot" moment, a sudden realization of a seemingly minute detail that would be the slender thread of solution.

• • •

Entering Jellicle's that evening, Kate spied Tri seated at a window booth, sipping his black coffee as he watched the busy intersection in front of the restaurant. He did not appear to be interested in the comings and goings of Fort Summit traffic, however. His pensive manner was that of a man deep in thought, perhaps contemplating the recent events of murder and intrigue, and how to put it all together in a series of gripping articles.

As soon as Kate slid into the seat opposite Tri, Ben arrived with briefcase in hand, still attired in a business suit.

"I hope I'm not late," he said, "I just came from the office. Something came up."

"I just got here, too," Kate said.

Ben sat down next to Tri, opened his briefcase and fumbled through papers. A waitress with black-and-white cat's ears protruding from a headband in her hair took beverage orders. Ben asked for a glass of merlot, Kate an iced tea. Tri just wanted a coffee refill.

"Ballistics came back. Pete was shot with a .38 revolver," Ben said, "registered to a Pete Fogel. He was killed with his own gun. There was no forced entry, although he was known to be careless about locking his doors." Ben's voice softened as he mulled over this last fact. "It doesn't make sense, though, to have a gun for protection and forget to lock your door."

"Perhaps he was passed out after a drinking binge."

"Perhaps."

After a short pause, Ben grabbed some sheets and said, "I've got copies of the phone logs, and I think you might find this information interesting. In the last few days of his life, Pete phoned Rick Schmidt, Joe Randolph and Larry Anders at least once. When police contacted the men, they all acknowledged that Pete had called them, but they denied that they saw him or even talked to him.

"On the probable evening of his death, Randolph said he was home with his wife. He said she'll testify to that. The senator drives a red Porsche and dresses to the nines. Schmidt was on the road, around Delaware and Maryland, but admits to spending a night in New Jersey, about a half hour from Fogel's place. He drives an Infiniti, dark blue, dresses nicely, too, according to his co-workers. Anders said he went nowhere; he was just working on his farm. This is a busy time of year for him, he said. However, there's no corroboration of that. His wife was out of town during that time, evidently helping her sick mother. He owns a brown Ford pickup; his wife drives a beige Chevy sedan."

"Did you check on Ralph?" Kate asked, feeling like a betrayer by merely posing the question.

"Yes, the kids he works with saw him both mornings on those days. But he could have driven to Pete's and gotten back by morning. You said he told you Pete called him about a month before he died? Phone records bear that out. Actually, it was about five weeks before. He owns a green Honda; his wife drives a white Buick.

"Oh, one more thing," Ben added. "Fogel called his sister, just two days before his death. She was shocked and horrified by her brother's murder; she really took the news hard. She said her brother wanted to visit her, get acquainted with his nieces and nephew, spend some time just catching up. She said he had a sense of urgency to his voice. This time, things would be different, he said. He would be different."

"What does that mean?" Kate asked.

"She wasn't really certain. She thought he sounded as

if he wanted to make things right in his life, as if he had some terrible secret that he wanted to talk about. He wasn't specific, she said, just said things like 'I need to come clean about my sins,' and 'I want to confess to God what I've done so I can be forgiven.'"

"Do you know if he spoke to a priest, pastor, rabbi, counselor, anybody about his secret?"

"The police are checking that out. But if he did confess to some crime, such as murder, his confession may not be able to be used in court. The only hope we have is that because Pete is dead, that information may be court evidence in his murder investigation."

"So what have we got here?" Tri asked. "Anything solid?"

"Nothing firm yet, but the police are going to have a serious conversation with Rick and Larry. Joe's leaving town tomorrow on a congressional trip to India. He'll be gone at least a week. Torrini will talk to him when he gets back."

"But it could be possible that Rick was the well-dressed man in the nice car who visited Pete, right? And maybe Larry got to Jersey and cabbed it, fearing that a pickup might attract too much attention."

"That's an interesting point, Tri. But in Pete's neighborhood, a pickup would attract less attention than an Infiniti. And someone dressed in work clothes is more commonplace than Mr. Fancy Pants."

"So we either have the cleverest of killers or a bumbler who got lucky out of sheer ignorance," Kate said.

Chapter Twelve

Kate relayed peripheral facts to Ralph about the murder investigation, who responded with an occasional "Uh-huh." Then he said, "It's hard to swallow that any of these guys would have killed Pete. But then, it's hard to believe that any one of them would have killed that girl.

"I'm stuck on Pete's words to his sister, though. They were similar to what he said to me, of course, but when I hear you repeat them, well, it makes Pete sound very guilty." Thinking out loud, Ralph said, "Even if Pete were involved with illegal drugs, what would that have to do with the girl? And how would that connect with his death? Do you think he killed the girl? Or perhaps he saw something happen, someone else kill the girl, and he was blackmailing that person?"

Then he blurted, "But that can't be. Pete had a wretched existence. If he was blackmailing someone, he wouldn't have lived like he did. He would've had money, cars, a nice home."

"You told me Pete was married once. Any idea how we could contact his ex?"

"I think she came from the Decker, Ind., area. Her name was Darla, or Diane. I think Rick might know more about her; they went to the same high school, although Rick was older." After a brief, thoughtful silence, Ralph asked, "Do you think Pete may have said something to her about the girl in Vietnam? About what happened that night?"

"Only if we're lucky," Kate said.

Before she called Rick, she jotted down a few piercing questions that she knew may not be answered, or may be answered falsely. Did you see Pete shortly before his death? Why did he call you? Did he have something to hide? Was he blackmailing anyone? Was he being blackmailed? What can you tell me about his former wife? Do you know where she could be located?

She dialed Rick's cell phone and got his message mailbox. Her first instinct was to hang up, assuming that if she left a message, he wouldn't call back. But she hesitated, deciding to give only her cell phone number. Rick might think she was a client.

Larry would be harder to talk to, she knew. His stonewalling attitude the first time she spoke with him displayed an insecurity that would never lead to honest apologetic reflection. She must be more artful in her approach this time.

Looking through her closet, she pulled out an ordinary slate-colored dress and decided on a plan of action. Because Larry didn't know what she looked like, she would visit his farm as the reporter she is. The paper is running a series of articles on Vietnam, she would explain, and she seeks some personal stories about that time. Maybe this way she could get some answers. She dialed the number and received a brusque "hello," then explained her purpose, quickly confirming the date and time.

Heading east to Ohio, she drove down Larry's muddy, rutted driveway, walked the broken, cracked sidewalk to the house and rang the doorbell.

• • •

"Hello, Mr. Anders, my name is Terri Olsen," said the young woman, dressed in a neutral gray outfit that was just a little too roomy for her slim frame. Her hair was pulled back in a ponytail, perhaps a bit too severely, and a pair of glasses rimmed the face that was unadorned with make-up.

"I am a reporter for *The Fort Observer*, and we are running a series of articles about the Vietnam War and our veterans. I understand that you served in Vietnam during that time. I won't take up much of your time, but I do have some questions. May I come in?"

"Okay."

She was ushered into a living room that bore the remnants of '70s decorating style and sat down on a floral slipcovered couch. Pulling out a reporter's tablet and pen, she set a handheld recorder and a file of papers on the coffee table.

Kate said, "Now, let's see, you were in Vietnam from January to December, 1969, is that correct?"

"Yes." Larry's smile was weak but warmer than his phone personality.

"In Charlie Company. Were you wounded?"

"Yeah, in the shoulder, when a land mine exploded about 20 feet away from me."

"Yes. I believe the man who stepped on it lost his life."

"His name was Holton."

"Do you have contact with anyone from C Company?"

"No. I never see them anymore."

"Any phone conversations?"

"No."

"We're looking for one man; his name is —," Kate pretended to shuffle through some papers, then triumphantly pulled one out, "Ah, yes, Fogel, Pete Fogel. Do you know where we can contact him?"

"No."

"And you haven't spoken with him, even on the phone?"

"Nope."

"There are some questions as to Mr. Fogel's service. Did he serve honorably, to the best of your knowledge?"

"I suppose so."

"Was Mr. Fogel involved in anything illegal that may mar his service record?"

A flicker of insider gossip darted in Larry's eyes as he moved his face closer.

"I heard tell he was involved with drugs — marijuana, coke, heroin. I never saw him use anything, though. I would've busted him. But that was the talk."

"How about anyone else in your platoon?"

"Rumor had it that someone else was Pete's partner."

"Any idea who?"

"Well, his drinking buddy was Ralph Sherman. I always figured they were in it together."

"Do you know if Mr. Sherman used drugs?"

"I knew he was a lush."

"Did you know Pete's former wife? Do you know where we could reach her?"

Larry's eyes narrowed as he bored a hard squint into Kate's. "What does this have to do with your article?"

"Oh, excuse me," Kate said breezily. "You see, Mr. Fogel passed away recently, and we thought we should at least let his former wife know that."

"I can't help you out there."

"Can you tell me what some of your experiences were in Vietnam?"

"Yeah. It was the worst time of my life. That's all I remember."

"Any instances that may have made you question your mission there?"

"The whole damn tour of duty made me do that."

"Could you give our readers some insights?"

"No." Larry stood up, pulled his pants up in back, sniffed, then said, "I think you better leave."

"Oh, uh, certainly, Mr. Anders. I-I didn't mean to take up your time. If you find out any more information about Mr. Fogel's former wife, please let me know." Kate gathered her file and recorder and neared the door. "Give your wife my regards, and have a good day."

Larry guided her to the entry, then said a curt "'Bye."

Kate went to her car, alone, then briefly smiled as she climbed inside. She watched Larry's stony face as he shut the door. Phone logs are a solid way to prove him a liar, she thought. There must be other information, too.

• • •

"It appears that Pete Fogel had a comrade, someone who helped him deal drugs," Kate reported to Tri. "Larry assumed it was Ralph."

"Larry assumed this because Ralph and Pete were drinking buddies?"

"Yes."

"Kate, I don't want you to investigate any more on your own. There's an undercurrent of danger about this whole thing."

"An undercurrent of danger?" Kate asked. "More like a conspiracy. It's almost as if, well, people are pulling the strings behind the scenes. It isn't just random evil."

Kate thought again of her father's death, a presumably chance "accident," unexplainable, everyone said, just another awful happening in this sad world. How could we know the mind of God? How could we possibly grasp the full meaning of life? It was hard enough to accept the unfathomable will of God, but what if her father's death was the will of others, sinister shadows who play God with the lives of all who get in their way? That she doubted she could accept — or forgive.

"Precisely why you are not to do this alone again," Tri admonished. "I talked to Ben today. He said there's some new information on the case. He asked us to meet him in his office after work."

In many ways, Ben reminded Kate of her father. He didn't look like Patrick, but Ben seemed to be a solid, straight-arrow kind of guy — smart, honest, without guise or deceit. With one exception, the few times she had met with him were serious occasions, involving legalities, court procedures, investigations, in which his behavior was appropriately sober.

Last Christmastime, however, Ben attended a newspaper party at the bidding of his reporter pal, Randy Thompson, Kate's fussy mother hen. Although the deputy prosecutor was a bit quieter than most of the reporters, and all of the sports writers, he displayed a penchant for wit and a dollop of self-deprecating humor that impressed Kate.

Of course, Ben had noticed the willowy strawberry blonde with the startling blue eyes. On the outside, she was kind, with a comfortable demeanor that generated warmth and goodness. But Ben perceived a stubbornness, too, that manifested itself with a strength and courage unusual to one so young. When he glimpsed her at the Christmas party, as often as he could without appearing to be staring, her easy laughter tingled inside him like sunshine bouncing off a glimmering lake.

Why he yet hadn't asked her on a date was a constant question in his mind. He told himself that he works such long hours and was concerned that the lovely, vibrant Kate may find him uninteresting. Although he yearned to travel to fascinating places, read a library of brilliantly written historical books, go whitewater rafting and learn how to pilot a plane, right now his life was a hamster's wheel of courts, cases and clients. Besides, he reminded himself, Kate had never shown any more attraction to him than simply as an acquaintance or, maybe, a friend. The latter caused a smile to cross his face. Anything more than that, he thought, would be hoping for too much.

• • •

The dark creases around Ben's eyes bore evidence of a long work week, but his voice was inviting as he bid the two to sit down.

"The New Jersey police have tracked down the taxi driver, the one who drove the shabby guy to Pete's. The cab driver picked this guy up two days before the body was found, according to the records," Ben said, rubbing his eyes. "That meshes with the coroner's estimate on the time of death.

"The driver said the guy looked pretty average — the kind of person he picks up all the time. There was nothing really distinguishing about him. A baseball cap hid most of his hair; his clothes were nondescript. He hunched himself on the seat so the cabby couldn't judge his height. He said the guy appeared nervous and sweating, though he did get a glimpse of his face. There was one thing, though, that caught the attention of the taxi driver. He was wearing a Rolex."

"Is the driver certain of that?" Kate asked.

"I questioned that, too," Ben said. "The driver was unclear about so many other descriptive points — height, weight, coloring — but of this one thing he is certain. He explained that he used to be a salesman in a swanky jewelry store until he got laid off. He notices watches, rings, that kind of thing. Says he's dead-bang certain this was a Rolex."

Chapter Thirteen

Kate was not close to Sam Owen, but she wanted to talk to him because he had known and respected her father. As managing editor, it wasn't unusual for reporters to speak with Sam privately about story difficulties, or even personal matters. Sometimes his door was open, inviting newspaper buzz or watercooler gossip, so when Kate entered shortly after lunch, Sam assumed it would be a business discussion.

Sam devoured the last bite of his sandwich and gulped the remains of a diet cola when Kate came in.

"Sam, can we talk?"

"Certainly," he said, "Kate, I want to commend you and Tri for your work on the Vietnam articles."

"Thanks. Tri is invaluable for his insight and personal experience."

"Have a seat."

Kate hesitated by the open door, uncertain of how to begin the conversation. Gently closing the door behind her, she stiffly sat down, back straight, hands clasped tightly in her lap.

"Is anything wrong?"

"No-no. I mean, everything is fine at work. I just -"

"Yes?"

"I would like to ask you some questions about my father."

Sam's eyebrows shot up; with a surprised look he said,

"All right."

"Particularly what my father was doing shortly before he died."

"What do you mean?"

"The envelope. I believe you must have placed it on my desk."

Sam leaned back in his chair and slumped, still staring at Kate. "I did."

"My dad was investigating an incident that occurred when he was in Vietnam — the murder of a young girl, possibly by someone in his unit."

"I didn't know the specifics, but he mentioned to me that he was trying to find some answers."

"Can you tell me anything about his last night?"

"Such as?"

"Such as why he was on Highway 3, where he was going and how he missed the turn by the bridge."

"Patrick was working on a murder trial, um, let's see, I think the name was Harris. This guy was married, had a child, and got involved with a teenager. She was pregnant, but the baby wasn't his. Police found her body in a tangle of brush near the Miami River. Patrick worked hard that day and was really tired, but he said he got a call from a guy in Sycamore who had a lead on the case. That's where he was going that night, to Sycamore."

"Do you know who this person might be? His name, phone number, anything?"

"If Patrick mentioned his name, I don't remember it. I

checked the phone logs after Patrick's death, and I couldn't find any calls from Sycamore, although the guy could have called from Fort Summit, I suppose."

"You were suspicious?"

Sam leaned forward and planted his elbows on his desk, looking squarely into Kate's eyes. "I was puzzled — and disturbed. Your father was familiar with that patch of road. I just didn't understand."

"You know that I have been checking into this Vietnam incident and that a man has been murdered. Do you think my father's, um, accident could have any connection with what he was investigating?"

"Kate, I don't know. This whole thing is very unsettling."

"Can you think of anything else that might shed some light on this matter?"

"Not right now, but I'll mull it over. I just ask that you be careful."

"I will. And if you find out anything more about my father's death or information about this case, please let me know."

"I'll do that, and you take care."

• • •

The call came on Kate's cell phone just as she was finishing an article about two women who were scamming churches by taking advantage of their good-hearted charity.

"May I speak to Sally Olsen, please?" asked an ebullient voice.

"Uh, yes, this is she," Kate responded, at first stumbling, then quickly recovering. "Who is this?"

"This is Rick Schmidt, marketing executive at Soy Green. May I help you?"

"Yes, Mr. Schmidt, thank you for returning my call. Could we meet tomorrow to talk?

"Certainly. Which company do you work for?"

"Foodfare Industries," Kate lied. "It's a fairly new company on the market."

"Okay. How about 11:30 tomorrow? Let's go to lunch."

"Fine. You choose the restaurant."

Rick chose an upscale Italian restaurant on the west end of town, not too far from the newsroom. Kate was glad she would have time to think about her questions and her approach. She decided that she would not engage in deceitfulness this time; she would be upfront, inform Mr. Schmidt who she was and what she wanted to know.

Perhaps Rick would be cooperative, and perhaps he wouldn't be, but Kate was certain that she couldn't be harmed by him, not in a restaurant full of people. Then her dismissive attitude turned dark. He could follow her, even stalk her. She must take care. Should Tri go, too? She was still weighing that option when Tri appeared by her computer.

"I found Pete Fogel's ex-wife," Tri said. "I called the high school and spoke to the secretary, Tammy. As luck would have it, she was in the same class as Pete's former wife, Darla." He placed a stub of paper on her

120

desk. "Here's her maiden name — Darla Beebe. She and Pete married young, shortly before he went to Vietnam. And when he got back, Darla realized she'd made a big mistake. The marriage fell apart within months. There were no children.

"Darla's remarried to a guy named Hovis, lives in Monroeville and has two children. Tammy said the last class reunion they had, Darla's daughter was expecting, so she's probably a grandmother. Care to go with me when I talk with her?"

Kate was thrilled with the invitation and responded with one in kind. "I'll go with you, and you can go with me on another interview. I've just spoken with Rick Schmidt. We're meeting tomorrow for lunch at Napoli's, 11:30. Are you interested?"

Tri's eyebrows shot up and his eyes sparkled as a broad grin spread across his face.

• • •

By the time the lunch crowd arrives at Napoli's, around noon, the line begins to form in the waiting area, often trailing to the outside door. Patrons usually wear tailored suits; the women display neatly manicured hands and well-coiffed hair. The restaurant would soon be buzzing with people and waiters precariously balancing oversized food trays on the fingers of one hand. But at 11:30, Kate and Tri were ushered to a table where the waiting Rick was sipping a fruit-blended iced tea. He stood briefly to shake hands with the two as Kate made introductions.

121

"Mr. Schmidt, this is my co-worker, Tri Nguyen. And I am Kate, Kate O'Riordan. We came to discuss a very urgent matter with you. I apologize for the original deception, but I very much wanted to meet with you."

Rick's warm smile diffused into a look of puzzlement, then understanding.

"O'Riordan. You're Patrick's daughter, aren't you? Yes, I can see a resemblance to your father around the eyes."

"I am. Again, I'm sorry for the deception. Tri and I have been working on this, uh, story for a few weeks, and it has taken some interesting turns. During the last two weeks of my father's life, he contacted several former Army buddies — you were one of them — to discuss a certain matter. I think it may have been the death of a young Vietnamese girl, caught by some in Charlie Company in a compromising position."

Rick's face displayed a tired anguish, and a bit of pique, during Kate's apologetic explanation, before he broke in.

"Many years ago, I spoke with your father about this same situation. I told him everything I knew, which wasn't much, but I thought this matter had been put to rest."

Placing his elbows on the table, he rubbed the sides of his nose with his index fingers, then tightly clasped his hands. The sleeves of his expensive jacket hiked up, just enough to display a pricey gold watch.

"Oh," Kate chimed in, "What a beautiful watch. Is it a

Rolex?"

"Yes," he replied, "It was given to me as a gift, for sales and service to the company. Tell me," he went on, "did your father ever find out the full story of what happened, uh, that night in Vietnam?"

"If he did, I have no knowledge of it. I only know of his investigation. Perhaps if he had lived longer ..."

Tri broke the pause with a question of his own.

"As I understand it, Mr. Schmidt, there were five of you who came upon the girl and her boyfriend. After the boy ran, um, well, can you tell us what occurred after that?"

"Someone said the girl had to be silenced. I think it was Larry who tied her wrists to the tree. Joe always carried a deck of cards, at least a euchre deck. He loved playing that game. Somehow it was decided that whoever got the ace of spades had to take care of the problem. I just know I didn't get the card, I didn't ask any questions, and I didn't harm that girl. I know I'm not much help, but I try never to think about it again." Rick's eyes glanced downward at the soft sheen of the table. "I haven't been successful with that either."

"Do you think one of the other four possibly killed the girl? We suspect that somebody did," Tri asked.

"It's hard to imagine any one of those guys doing that, even during a war. I really don't know what happened. I don't want to know."

"Shortly before his death, Pete Fogel called you," Kate said. "After all these years, what did he want? What did he say?"

"Pete was a guy with a lot of problems. He was often drugged, usually drunk, depressed as hell. I guess we all were depressed. But Pete, well, Pete just couldn't bounce back. He told me he'd been in and out of jail, said his whole life was a waste. He'd never been able to get into the mainstream of things.

"Yeah, he wanted to talk to me about that night. He told me to meet him at Dino's Pizza at 9:00. I drove all day to get there, but he didn't show; I waited for about a half hour. When he didn't come, I drove over to his apartment."

With a long sigh, he placed an index finger on his mouth, then looked at Kate as he spoke.

"I parked near the front of the apartment and walked up the stairs. The door was closed, but it wasn't locked. The place was completely dark. I walked inside, slowly, carefully. Things just didn't seem right."

He shifted in his seat, hesitantly gazed up at the ceiling, then continued.

"When I got to the bedroom, I turned on the light and, well, I saw Pete lying there dead. He looked like he'd just been killed; his body was warm. My God, when will this end? I panicked. I doused the light, and I left as quietly, and as quickly, as I could."

"Did you close the door?" Kate asked.

"Yes. Funny that I would think of that. I wiped the knob with my handkerchief. I know that sounds guilty, but —

"All I want to do is forget about all of this, and now Pete shows up dead. Someone killed him — I didn't!" Rick's look was pleading, but he soon collected himself. With a dismissive gesture, he said, "I don't know if Pete's death had anything to do with Vietnam. He probably made an enemy somewhere along the way who caught up with him. Pete was always on the fringe."

"What did Pete want to talk to you about? You and the others?"

"He wanted to talk about the girl, something that only he knew about, or maybe he and someone else."

"Did Pete have anything to hide, personally, about his behavior that night? Or was he blackmailing someone because of something he saw?" Kate asked.

"I told you, I never got a chance to talk to him. He didn't say much on the phone, just that he wanted to see me personally. I don't know what he knew about that night, but he knew something. Otherwise, why would he want to talk to me about it? As for blackmail, he would be capable of it, but people who blackmail have a far better life than Pete had."

That does make sense, Tri mused, then said, "Pete's former wife, Darla, went to the same high school as you. What can you tell me about her?"

"Very little. I know who she was, but she was younger than me. I really never spoke to her."

"Any idea where she could be located?" Tri knew the answer to this question, but he decided to ask it anyway.

"I have no idea, but it shouldn't be difficult to track

125

her down. I'd start with the high school."

"Did anyone see you leave Pete's place? Did you see anyone?" Kate asked, ignoring his previous remark.

"I saw no one. I don't think anyone saw me."

"Actually, someone did see you," Tri broke in. "Three people, in fact. You took a cab; do you remember the name of the cab company?"

"I didn't take a cab. I told you, I drove there."

"What make of car did you drive?"

"My car. It's an Infiniti, navy blue. You say three people saw me?"

"Well, they didn't exactly see your face, but they were impressed with your car."

"Then why did you think I took a cab?"

"I must have been mistaken."

"There's something else, isn't there? Someone took a cab there? Was it before I arrived or after? Did anyone get a description of the guy?"

"Actually, the cab driver was unclear about a lot of things — height, weight," Tri said. "He said the man wore a ball cap so he wasn't positive about hair color either. There was one thing he was certain about, though. The guy was sporting a Rolex."

Chapter Fourteen

Darla Hovis had graying hair and tired eyes that displayed a worldly wisdom borne of experience. Although she was thoughtful and intelligent, her family's meager circumstances, and low expectations for their children, had crushed the dreams she held close to her heart. If she had wanted to be a schoolteacher or a nurse, her parents may have been able, and willing, to support her desire as best they could. But Darla's imaginings were far more boundless.

She remembered lying on soft tufts of grass in the field next to her house, watching clouds meander on their gauzy trail. Someday, she convinced herself, she would journey like that, all over the world, see things, do things, experience life and living in a large way. But how does one balance such vaunted dreams into the ordered book-and-study world of college?

She was 19 when she married Pete; he was 20, a mechanic with yearnings that matched her own. They would travel the world, he promised, by working and backpacking their way across Europe, then head to other exotic places and destinations all over the globe.

Darla was certain she had found her soul mate, someone whose gut ached for adventure, the dramatic stuff of life, the spirit of which was like a maelstrom inside her that could not be stilled. She often wondered why God, or the fates, had ignited such passion in her soul, then shackled her in such stultifying circumstances.

Years ago, she filed those reveries in the attic of her mind. Yet, even now, as a mother of two grown children and a grandmother, she would gingerly revisit those aspirations, allowing an occasional shard of sunlight to dance across her dreams. The regret in her heart didn't ache so much now; the gentle tugs of yearning had become ephemeral friends who no longer taunted her. Certainly, her adventurous spirit would never dissipate, only mellow with time and age and reality.

And when she thought of Pete returning from Vietnam, drug-addicted, depressed, barely able to sleep or eat because of things he saw and did in that horrible war, Darla felt her dreams washing away as quickly as sand under her feet in a swift undertow.

• • •

Kate and Tri pulled up to a green, black-shuttered two-story that was tucked away on a side street in Monroeville. A few clusters of crocuses peaked through the mulch along the sidewalk. Because her husband worked the third shift in the local plastics factory, he was asleep when the two arrived to talk around 10:00 a.m.

They were ushered in to the home's tidy kitchen, an inviting area with a colorful border that nestled along the chair line.

"Would you like some coffee? I just made a fresh pot," Darla said.

Tri accepted her offer, but Kate declined. Darla gave a steaming mug to Tri, then placed the other mug in front of her as she sat down to talk.

"Mrs. Hovis," Kate began, but was interrupted by a kind but firm voice. "Darla. You can call me Darla."

"Darla, I'm sure you've heard about what happened to your former husband. However, our questions will concern the brief time you knew Pete and were married to him."

Darla nodded her head in understanding.

"When he came back from Vietnam, was anything different about him? Did he ever share any stories about things that happened during the war, about Charlie Company?"

Darla's eyes were downcast, gazing into her cup, grasping it with both hands as she contemplated the questions.

"At first, I thought Pete had changed a lot after Vietnam," she pondered. "He was on edge, depressed, he slept fitfully, he couldn't eat. He complained constantly about the way people at home treated him because he was a Vietnam vet. Actually, many people were kind and respectful, but he zeroed in on those few who called him a baby killer — or a sucker for fighting for his country. Mostly, they were young kids, antiestablishment hippie types, who were so smug in their own self-righteous attitudes that —" Darla caught herself, remembering the bad times with the same bitterness that Pete spat out.

"Anyway, as I've had time to mull things over, I realize that the seeds of instability were always in Pete. He'd had a very unhappy childhood, although I always liked his sister. Perhaps the war brought out the worst in him, but I'm not sure if, with or without Vietnam, he wouldn't have taken a similar path."

"Do you know where his sister could be reached? Do you remember what her married name is?" Tri asked.

"Her name is Jackson, Sally Jackson. I'm sorry to say that I have completely lost touch with her. For a couple of years after the divorce, we talked occasionally and sent cards at Christmas, but, well, I remarried, she moved, and our correspondence stopped. I think she still lives in southern Indiana, but I'm not positive."

• • •

It was around noon when Tri and Kate left Darla's house; the sun radiated its bright aura through thick, gusty clouds.

"Let's put together what we have here," Tri said, and Kate agreed, explaining that she had already begun doing so. "But it always helps to organize thoughts with another person," she added. "You start."

"Well, let's go through the five people involved in that fateful night — Larry, Rick, Ralph, Joe and Tom. Joe dealt the cards; Ralph got the card. Ralph told Pete, making him a sixth suspect. Tom died — he's not a suspect — but the others are, including Pete. He may have been shot because he killed the girl, or he saw who did. If he saw who did, why wouldn't he turn that

130

person in to authorities — or resort to blackmail?"

Tri stopped, pondering this last supposition. "Unless, of course, that person wasn't wealthy. But if he couldn't get money, then why wouldn't he turn him in?"

"The buddy code?" Kate asked.

"Could be. Or was Pete killed to be silenced or to stop the blackmail?" His thoughts ran ahead of his words. "But how could Pete be a blackmailer, living like he did? And why would he have remained silent all these years about what happened?"

"Perhaps the girl's killer had some other hold on Pete. Rumor was that Pete was dealing drugs. Maybe the killer had evidence of that; maybe that's why Pete didn't talk. You turn me in; I'll turn you in."

"That explains his silence, for awhile. Rick, Joe and Ralph have done well financially. Was he trying to shake down the girl's killer now, after all these years?"

"Could be. Let's go back to the night of Pete's death. All four men — Larry, Joe, Rick or, uh, Ralph —," Kate hesitated on the last name, "could be his killer. We know that Rick was there and drives a dark, high-priced car. He wears a Rolex. He could have taken a taxi to kill Pete, then changed clothes and drove back to Pete's to support his story."

"But why wouldn't he have made certain he was seen and heard the second time? Why would he have left so secretly?"

"Good question. Okay. Joe says he was home. He dresses smartly, drives the big car. I don't know if he has a Rolex, but he probably has expensive jewelry. Would he have killed Pete because of what happened in Vietnam?"

Kate thought of blackmail, then said, "Joe would have been the perfect blackmail target, especially after his father's death. He's the wealthiest one of these men. Yet, that doesn't explain Pete's poverty."

"Larry may own a Rolex, though I doubt it," Tri mused, but remembering his meeting with Rick, he said, "Rick certainly wears one, and we know he was at Pete's on the night of the murder. But was Larry? We must find out if the police have found any credit-card receipts on that night, or someone who may remember Larry at a restaurant or gas station. An eyewitness or a paper trail, anything that can help us."

"We also need to find out what the police know about Larry's finances. He may have far more money than it appears."

"Mm, hmm."

"And there's just so much about Pete we don't know. Perhaps no one does." Kate peered out of the car window, watching clouds dapple the sunlight on the wet earth.

• • •

Returning to work, Kate found a note, tucked neatly under her keyboard, that Ben had called. She dialed the number and was surprised when Ben picked up.

"Ben, hello. I expected an answering machine, or your secretary."

132

"My secretary's at lunch," he said, "so I'm just eating at my desk."

"I'm glad you can talk. Anything new on the case?"

There was more information, he said, some very informative, some that added even more mystery to the enigmatic Pete.

"I appreciate your help, Ben," Kate said, while twisting her phone cord around her index finger. It always seemed to be a curl or two out of kilter. "Could we meet after work, with Tri, to discuss this new information over coffee?"

The two decided on a little coffee house in mid-downtown Fort Summit, a throwback to the beatnik days of the '50s, a collection of boutiques, antique stores and small spaces where artists, crafters, quilters, candle makers and glass blowers could ply their trade.

The coffee house, "Grounds for Cause," featured poetry readings with bongo music, budding singers and songwriters, and a collection of local art and sculptures, contemporary and country.

Tri and Kate arrived first, and found a solitary table tucked into a shadowed corner, where the three could quietly discuss new information in the case. Ben joined them within five minutes. He was carrying a briefcase tightly closed on a sheaf of paper, something he shoved in just before he left his office.

"There's some very interesting developments about this case," Ben said as he placed his briefcase on the table and opened it with a snap. He slid into the booth

133

next to Kate and continued his comments.

"A waitress from a little eatery in Plainfield recognized a photo of Larry. She said she doesn't pay too much attention to her customers' appearance, but this guy was alone. He complained about his hamburger, he griped about the wait, and then he didn't leave a tip. If you want to go unnoticed, you shouldn't be difficult to your waitress. Oh, and he was wearing a baseball cap, jeans and boots."

"When was this?" Tri asked.

"It was about two hours before Pete's death. No one, however, remembers if he was driving a car or a truck. Regardless, he could have cabbed it."

"Does Larry have the money for blackmail?" Kate drew her eyebrows together pensively. "Is there any money trail?"

"None that has been found, and, no, Larry doesn't appear to be as well off as the other three suspects. But investigators couldn't find a money connection with Rick, Ralph or Joe either. From time to time, Joe has withdrawn cash, sometimes of rather large amounts. There's one for $10,000 in March 1975, another $10,000 in January 1981 and $25,000 in July 1989. This might look bad for a senator, but, being a politician, well, I've seen many things go on in the political arena."

"But Joe wasn't a senator until 1984," Kate interjected.

"Yes, but sometimes palms have to be greased along the way." Ben looked into Kate's eyes, their bright blue color darkened by the dim lights. "Look, I'm not condoning payoffs. I'm simply stating the facts about politics and the political system."

"Were there any deposits in Pete's account for those amounts near those dates?"

"No, none that the police could find, although they're still looking into it. It's puzzling, but investigators say there's very little activity in Pete's bank account. He opened the account with $25 two years ago and did little with it for almost three years, occasionally adding small amounts. He didn't deposit his checks, he didn't transfer money, he didn't open up another account. And this has been his pattern wherever he lived. Always a small amount, the minimum, perhaps, to open an account, then he'd let it sit.

"He earned about $20,000 a year at the quarry, cashed his weekly paychecks and took all of it with him. Living the way he did, he couldn't have spent it all. He smoked — a lot — and, for years, he drank too much, but that still doesn't explain why he had almost nothing to his name. The police are looking into secret bank accounts, some sort of paper trail, that may shed light on this. But so far, nothing."

After a brief pause, Tri said, "So we have three clear suspects, all of whom had motive, means and opportunity."

"There is no evidence of Joe being in Plainfield on the night of the murder," Ben said.

"But he could have been there and not at home as he said."

135

"There's always that possibility."

Chapter Fifteen

Larry Anders saw the police car advance to the house from inside his barn. Momentarily, he considered hiding, fleeing, whatever he could do to avoid the discussion that was about to be pressed on him. Instead, he strode toward the cruiser, mouth tight, eyes staring straight ahead, a little man with a big attitude.

"Officers, what's this all about?"

The officers stopped the car, got out and displayed their badges.

"Mr. Anders, I'm Detective Hobart and this is Detective Werling. We have several questions to ask you. You can either answer them here, or we'll take you in."

"What questions?"

"You told investigating officers that you were not in Plainfield on the night of Pete's murder, but we have evidence that you were. Your waitress at the Grill Shack identified your photo, said she was positive it was you. Care to comment?"

"Okay, I was there — but I didn't kill Pete."

"What were you doing in Plainfield?"

"Pete called a couple of days before he — died. Told me to meet him at 9 at some pizza place."

"So why didn't you?"

"I had nothing to do with anything."

"Pete thought you did."

"Pete was screwed up."

"What time did you leave the restaurant?"

"I don't know; I guess about 9:20."

"Why'd you leave?"

"I told you. I had nothing to do with it, and I didn't want to see anyone else."

"Where'd you go?"

"I drove around. I figured I'd talk to Pete alone, later. I just wanted him to leave me out of this whole thing."

"You were on the raid in Vietnam the night the girl was killed."

"Yeah. There were five of us, and Ralph blabbed to Pete when he got back, so that makes six. But I don't know what happened to the girl, and I don't know who killed Pete."

"What kind of car were you driving?"

"My pickup."

"Did anybody see you or your car at Pete's on the night of the murder?"

"I don't know. I parked down the street and walked to Pete's."

"How did you know his address?"

"He told me."

"Why walk? Why didn't you just drive there?"

"I told you. I just wanted to talk to Pete alone."

"And did you?"

Larry crossed his arms on his chest and lodged his tongue in his right cheek.

"No. When I got to Pete's place, I saw a car pull in. I

think it was Rick. I hid behind the building. He went upstairs to Pete's place, then left shortly after that."

"Did he see you?"

"No."

"Why did you hide?"

"I didn't want to talk to him."

"Did you hear anything, like a gunshot?"

"Hell, no. That bat who lives below had the TV on so loud it would wake the dead."

"Did you see Pete after that?"

Larry hesitated, his eyes peered far away, then returned to the face of Officer Hobart.

"I-I did go upstairs. The door was unlocked, and the place was dark. I called Pete's name, but no one answered, so I left."

"Did you see Pete?"

"No. I didn't look around at all. I was kinda creeped out."

"Your fingerprints weren't found on the doorknob."

"I used my handkerchief."

"Why?"

"Instinct, I guess. Cover your ass. That's what I learned in the Army."

"Did anyone else come?"

"Not that I know of."

"Did you see a cab?"

"Nope."

"Did you see Joe Randolph?"

"Uh-uh."

"Have you talked to Rick or Joe after that night?"

"Of course not."

Detective Hobart put his right hand on his hip, glaring through the darkness of his sunglasses. Detective Werling, the younger of the two, shifted nervously, looking down at the weeds and mud and stones.

"I'm sure we'll have more questions, Mr. Anders, so don't leave town."

"I'll try not to."

Chapter Sixteen

Peg Miller had been a teller for Plainfield National Bank for seven years, right after she graduated from high school. She was taking night courses in banking and business accounting at the community college with the hope that she would advance to an executive level.

She often waited on the scruffy guy who came in periodically with a bundle of cash to deposit. Sometimes he would only have a few hundred dollars. Other times he would have more than a thousand. She had lots of questions, such as where he got the money, why he didn't spend some on himself and why his only address was a post office box. But it wasn't her place to investigate; he was depositing the money, after all, not taking it out of his account.

He wasn't rude, but he spoke very little. His eyes were usually downcast, his face at least two days away from a razor. When he approached the window, his grimy fingers would reach into his front pants pocket and carefully hand the wadded money to the teller. Everyone has a story to tell, Peg knew, but this man's story would surely be a heartbreaker.

When he didn't show up at the bank for a couple of weeks, Peg didn't actually miss him. He didn't come in regularly at a certain time of a certain day, but events soon to unfold would jog her memory about when she had last seen the grizzled guy at the teller's window.

On a Wednesday evening, returning from one of her classes, she turned on the television to catch the news. A man had been murdered in Plainfield, and police were seeking any tips or information about the case. She finished dishing herself a scoop of ice cream when his picture appeared on the screen.

"My lord!" she said out loud. "That's Mr. Jackson!"

Peg grabbed a pencil and a used envelope, writing the number down in a hurriedly scrawled manner. Her hand shook as she dialed the number, fumbling with her words when a voice on the other end offered assistance.

"This is the Plainfield Police Department. May I help you?"

"Yes, I think. I mean, I think I know the man who was killed. His name was Jackson, Pete Jackson. He came into my bank, I mean, not my bank, but …"

"Ma'am, we have no record of a Pete Jackson being killed."

"I know. That was the name he went by. But the picture of the man who was killed, um, Pete Fogel, I'm certain that's Mr. Jackson. He has an account at the bank where I work."

"You think Mr. Fogel had an account at your bank?"

"Yes, but he went by Jackson, Pete Jackson."

"Give me your name and phone number, and I'll have a detective call you tomorrow morning."

• • •

The president of Plainfield National Bank was

142

deferential when police investigators and Prosecutor Torrini met with him. He was shocked, he said, to hear of the violent death of one of his patrons. He led the group to the bank records, jabbering about the upstanding establishment of his bank and how such an incident had never before occurred.

Several other accounts, listed under the Jackson name in cities where Pete formerly lived followed the same pattern: two banks, two bank accounts — the Fogel name with a minimal balance and the Jackson name with an amount that continued to grow, sometimes with large deposits. It better explained what Mr. Fogel did with the money he earned and received by other means. In addition to a substantial bank account, investigators found a safe-deposit box.

Chapter Seventeen

Sally Blanton was unlocking the door to her house when she heard the phone. She quickly tossed the mail and paper on the kitchen table and dashed to answer it.

"Mrs. Blanton?" the voice on the line queried.

"Yes."

"This is Anthony Torrini. I am prosecuting the case that involves your brother's murder."

"Yes. Do you have any new information?"

"Your brother left a safe-deposit box in a Plainfield, N.J., bank under an assumed name, but upon his death, ownership becomes yours. Could you come to New Jersey so the box can be opened? There's also a substantial amount of money that your brother left you. The prosecutor's office will pay for your travel expenses."

"Pete had money? He had a safe-deposit box? I had no idea."

"Evidently, he hid it well."

"I can come."

• • •

Officer Steve Rainey read the accident report again, checked on the license plate number and found it all very curious. On the night of Pete's murder, Dick Stevens exited a bar, albeit a little tipsy, and saw a light-colored compact back into a sports car. He called to the car's driver, but the compact sped away, leaving a fist-sized dent and streaks of paint on the Porsche's sleek exterior.

According to the report, Stevens said he went back in the bar and told the bartender, who informed everyone in the establishment about what happened. No one claimed the car as theirs, so the bartender called the police, who filed a report that ended up on the desk of Officer Rainey. He decided to call Prosecutor Torrini about the matter; he was certain he would be interested.

"Tony, this is Steve Rainey. I've got a little information here that I think might interest you."

"Shoot." The pun did not go undetected.

"Well, there was a fender-bender on the evening of June 23 at Bucky's, over on Leech Street. The front side of a sports car got hit by another car; a patron saw the whole thing. The car didn't belong to anyone in the bar, and no one saw who drove it off the lot — or when. But here's the kicker: The car is registered to a U.S. Senator from Indiana, and he's never filled out an accident report on it."

"What time did this happen?"

"Around 8:55."

"Let me guess. The senator's name is Joe Randolph."

"You got it."

"Send me the information and thanks for the heads up."

Torrini cupped his hands under his chin and pondered this new information. He would have several questions for the good senator, he thought, just as soon

146

as he returns from his overseas junket. Then he called
Ben Stuart and filled him in on this latest development.

• • •

Sally arrived at the Plainfield National Bank and
entered the office of the bank's president, where he,
Torrini and Ben Stuart were seated. The men rose when
she entered and, after exchanging names and
handshakes, the president showed her the bank account
and the box.

"Will you open it?" she asked the prosecutor.

The bank president handed the key to Torrini, who
deftly unlocked the box as the group gathered around
the long, black-metal enclosure.

Inside were Pete's Army dog tag, a childhood photo of
Pete and Sally, a faded picture of Darla in wedding
attire, a few old coins and a sealed letter. The envelope
said "For Sally's eyes only — on the event of my death."

"Read it to me," Sally said.

Torrini picked up the envelope and broke its seal with
his pocketknife. He began to read, out loud, to the
anxious group:

"Sally,

"I know I have disappointed you. I have disappointed
myself even more. Perhaps the seeds of failure were
sown in me long before Vietnam — I don't know; I'm
not much for introspection — but something happened
there that I can't forget, that set in motion a lifetime of
grief.

"One night, Tom, Joe, Rick, Larry and Ralph went on a

night excursion to find an enemy encampment. I was just getting over a bout of dysentery, so I stayed behind. Ralph and I had become buddies, mostly drinking buddies, but I liked him. He returned that night so drunk he could barely walk, but he needed to talk, and I was there.

"He said they came upon a couple, in the act. The boy ran; the girl didn't. She was too frightened to run, Ralph said. I know this is hard to understand; Ralph wept like a baby when he told me, but in the aloneness of war, wives and girlfriends seem unreal and far away. We were just so lonely. We wanted, needed, someone to make love to; it's a physical release.

"That poor girl, they all raped her, then decided they had to get rid of her. They drew cards, and Ralph got the card — the ace of spades. He was a mess. After the others took off, he decided he couldn't kill the girl, so he cut her bindings and let her go. At least, he thought he let her go.

"After Ralph told me this, then passed out, I went back to where he said he left the girl. I found her, and I found her killer, too. Joe Randolph was leaning over her body; he had broken her neck. When he saw me he told me to keep my mouth shut. He knew about the drug ring I was involved in, and he said he would report me for dealing in drugs and for killing the girl.

"Who would believe my word over his, he said. And he was right. Even then, I was on the edge. I helped him bury her in a tangle of undergrowth, and I swore to myself I would never think about it again. I know now that something stuffed that deep has been a cancer in my soul I could never destroy. Instead, it destroyed me.

"Through the years, Joe helped me out of a couple of scrapes with the law and gave me money a few times, too. I thought he owed me. Hell, I thought the whole world owed me. I was so immersed in guilt and self-pity I missed my entire life.

"A few years later, Joe asked me to help him out. He was running for senator, and he told me that there was a guy who was threatening to kill him. I asked him why someone would want to kill him, and he said the guy had a lot of money tied up in his opposing candidate and couldn't afford for him to lose.

"He asked me to get rid of him, make it look like an accident so no one would be suspicious. He said the guy would be traveling on State Road 3 on a hot July night. He said, drive a truck, a heavy one, and run him off the road before you reach the bridge.

"I told him I wasn't a killer — well, maybe in Vietnam I was. He said I still owed him for all the times he'd gotten me out of jail and out of trouble. He promised me he'd pay me $100,000 if I did it right.

"I swear to God, Sally, I didn't know it was Pat. I found out the next day when I heard the news. I felt betrayed, and I called Joe as hot as hell. But Joe is smooth, very smooth. He knew exactly what to say and how to say it. He could twist things, make it look as if I had a grudge against Pat. Who would believe a loser like me? And then he upped the payment to $150,000.

"My guilt has been overwhelming. I murdered my innocent friend for 30 pieces of silver. I knew I couldn't enjoy the money, so I've been saving it, and more, to give to you and your family.

"Lately, I've been trying to get straight. I went to a pastor and confessed everything. He encouraged me to talk to the police, make a clean slate of things so I could start a new life. I decided he was right, but first I called Joe, then Ralph, Rick and Larry. I wanted to talk to them before I went to the authorities. I know Joe has the most to lose and may even kill me. Frankly, I don't care if he does. That's why I'm writing this letter to you, to be opened after my death.

"I will let the police sort out the particulars on how I died. Chances are, Joe had his hand in it. More importantly, I want you to know that I am forgiven by God, and I'm still working on forgiving myself. I have never known such peace. Even prison can't hurt me now.

"I've always loved you and admired you. You are the kind of person I wish I had become. You may not be rich or famous, but you certainly are successful. You have love and goodness, joy and laughter, peace and kindness, family and good friends. All of life's truly greatest gifts, you have.

"Give my love to Mike and the kids. I'm sorry I wasn't a better brother or uncle. But now I know this — I will see you in eternity.

"God bless you all,

"Pete"

Sally was quietly weeping when Torrini read the letter, then she collapsed into long, hard sobs, wracking her shoulders, her hands enclosed over her face. The men remained quiet until she composed herself. She pushed her hair back from her face and dabbed at her eyes.

"I'm sorry," she said, "This is very difficult. Thank you for your help."

The men rose and responded with soothing murmurs. The bank president assured her that he would be of service to her in every way he could, then escorted her out of the bank.

Chapter Eighteen

Although Sen. Randolph's office was sometimes disordered, even chaotic, office manager Jane Reese was calm and organized, a cool glass of water on a sizzling day. She had been the senator's right-hand person since the beginning, when he, a newly elected member on the D.C. scene, and she, an experienced 20-something who had worked for a congressman who lost his election bid, decided to join forces and capture the hill.

Jane was not a great beauty, but she was not unattractive either. More than anything, she oozed confidence, intelligence and a no-nonsense disposition that completely suited her. Her formerly dark brown hair, now a honey blonde to cover the strands of gray that persisted at the temples, was blunt cut at the nape of her neck, allowing her straight hair minimal movement.

She stayed within five pounds of her youthful weight, the result of strict dieting and a self-designed workout regimen. She dressed handsomely, but never succumbed to fashion fads, the garish, over-sexualized apparel seen on the young and those vainly attempting to appear so. And she would never submit to tattoos or body piercing, other than the single hole in each of her earlobes.

She preferred fitted suits, belted dresses, pump heels, no "animal" prints, attractive but sensible jewelry, and no chunky bracelets. They were annoying to a busy office manager who didn't like the clink of wrist wear, its up-and-down movement on her arms, or the way they hampered her writing for quick note-taking.

Jane was, as usual, the competent overseer of the senator's bustling office who provided him with more than order, competency and loyalty. She worked late hours with the senator, ate with him, drank with him and shared his bed. Their agreement worked for both of them: She wanted employment and the DC life. He wanted the façade of devoted family man to keep his position.

• • •

A single tear trickled down Kate's cheek and moistened the page of the diary, her mother's diary, that she found among her parents' belongings. The unmarked dusty box had been put in storage for too long, Kate thought, and it was time to get it out. The cover was worn, and its binding was almost in tatters. It was only two years of Emily's brief life, but it was a window into her mother's heart and soul.

"I pray daily that I will find a good man, have his children and set right the bonfire that is my family," Emily wrote. "I want my marriage to be successful, and I want my children to know the God Who made them."

"Oh, mommy, I wish you were here," Kate said with deep, heaving sobs. "I so wish daddy was here, too."

Kate's mother's brother and divorced grandmother lived in Florida, emotionally farther away than the miles of distance between them. Her uncle, Doug, fathered a child with a woman who afforded him fleeting pleasure, although he was married to another at the time. The last Kate spoke to him, about eighteen months ago, he was between marriages, living with a woman who provided sexual outlet, clean laundry and home-cooked dinners. If the woman pressured too hard for the M word, as others did, she would be easily replaced with fresher, more naïve stock.

Kate's maternal grandmother lived alone. After two failed marriages, she tried cohabiting with a string of men, none of whom provided her with the security and love she desperately sought. She resigned herself to caring for her three cats and a collection of African violets.

Her maternal grandfather, who died three years earlier, had been married to his fourth wife, a much younger woman who inherited the beach house at his death. He had set aside some money for Kate, but the marriages and divorces had depleted that sum considerably.

Reading her mother's diary illuminated so much about her mother. Emily, born in the fragments of this household, determined at age seven that she would grow up to make things right with mom and dad and Doug. She especially loved stories of families who worked together during hard times — Laura Ingalls Wilder's "The Little House on the Prairie" books, "Little Women" and "The Five Little Peppers and How They

Grew" — united in love and devotion to each other, each considering the strength of marriage and family as more important than individual wants or desires. And she yearned that, someday, she would have this for herself and her children.

Kate understood too well the feelings of abandonment, loss, the injustice of life. And she, too, yearned for a loving marriage, children, a family. So many of the young men she dated were focused on other matters, and she couldn't picture herself with them, at least not in a lifelong situation.

When Kate first found out about her father's death, she couldn't talk about it, not even with a counselor. Her grandparents were loving people who would do anything for her, but they, too, were grieving — first their beloved daughter-in-law, then their only son. It was almost too much to bear. And yet, slowly, hourly, daily, life goes on. Each day presents enough difficulty of its own. And each day, they sought the peace and comfort of God; even if they didn't always feel it, they trusted in God's promises. *I am with you always, even to the ends of the earth.*

Kate clutched the dog-eared diary to her breast, reliving the times of great sorrow that had befallen her family. *Why God, why?* she asked.

• • •

The jangling phone intruded upon her grief. She hesitated before picking it up; what if it was a solicitor? On the third ring, she gingerly cradled the phone to her ear, answering with a soft hello.

"Kate? Hi. This is Ben. I have some news on the case, something that I need to talk to you about."

"Okay. Does this concern Pete's murder?"

"Yes. May I come over tonight, just for awhile? This isn't something I can explain over the phone. It's really important."

"Certainly. I'll be here."

Kate looked at her puffy eyes and red cheeks. I look a mess, she thought to herself. She washed her face in cold water, applied a little fresh makeup and ran a comb through her hair. When she heard a light tap on the apartment door, she invited Ben in.

Although he still bore his briefcase, he was dressed casually and his hair was a bit mussed.

"I got a call from Torrini tonight," he said. Kate thought he looked tired. "There's been a break in the case, and I think it's blown wide open."

"Talk to me."

"On the evening of Pete's death, there were three former Army buddies who were near or at Pete's house. Larry Anders wasn't at the pizza place, but he admitted to driving near Pete's place that night and walking the rest of the way. He said he drove his truck, and he saw someone — well dressed — who walked up to Pete's place. He thought the guy looked like Rick Schmidt, he said. Schmidt admits to waiting at the pizza place, then heading to Pete's house, probably around 9:20. He saw Pete, but he was already dead. When Schmidt left,

Anders came up, too. He said he called out Pete's name, but no one answered, so he left. The third man, the one who came in a cab, arrived before 9. We think he is the killer.

Kate felt a cold chill go through her body. "Go on," she said.

"On that evening, June 23, a car accident occurred at a bar named Bucky's. It was nothing serious. A driver pulled out and hit the fender of a sports car." Ben paused and took a deep breath. "The auto was registered to Joe Randolph. I'm sorry, Kate. Torrini said it happened around 8:55."

"And where was Joe?"

Ben cast his eyes on the floor. "It appears that he called a cab. The cabbie picked this guy up at a warehouse parking lot, then drove him to Pete's place, before 9." His gaze returned to Kate. "The driver said he looked pretty average, other than the Rolex, but he did get a quick look at his face. He picked Joe's photo out of several handed to him. He said he thinks Joe was the guy he drove to Pete's that night."

Kate sat limply, her right hand rubbed her forehead as hot tears stung her eyes. She felt Ben's arms around her, holding her gently. He was quiet for a while, then said in a soft, sad voice, "There's more."

Kate blinked hard. "I'm listening."

"Torrini told me that Pete had another bank account under the name of Jackson — Pete Jackson. He found out about it when a bank teller called in and recognized

Pete's face on TV news. Pete stashed a lot of money in this account, much of it probably obtained illegally through bribes. And there was a safe deposit box. It contained a few items of no significance to the investigation, but there was one key item: a letter written by Pete to his sister."

Ben clutched Kate just a little tighter.

"I'm sorry to tell you this, but," Ben paused and took in a deep breath, "He admits to killing your father."

"No!"

"Pete insisted he didn't know it was your father. He said Joe paid him to do it."

Kate buried her face in Ben's shirt, weeping softly, her arm around his neck. Ben felt the softness of her hair, the fresh, sweet smell of soap, the clutch of her hand on his back. He was not adept at comforting; he dealt with the law and its facts. He knew how to nail a guilty perp, he could navigate the mazes of the judicial system, and he respected smart detective work. But holding a sobbing woman, well, he just wasn't sure what to do. So he hugged her tightly, stroked her hair, found himself saying "I'm sorry; I'm so sorry. It will be all right."

• • •

The senator was expecting the call that morning, but he was hoping to delay it. Jane picked up the call and directed it to Joe's "inner sanctum," a private area that abutted the oak-paneled office, where few have been invited.

Joe canceled his early meeting with the Friends of

India delegation, whom he was scheduled to address later that day. He was in his office with his lawyer, discussing in hushed tones how to handle this latest bombshell — the car traced to him that was parked at the bar on the night of the murder.

He picked up the phone and said, "This is Senator Randolph."

"Good morning, Senator. This is Anthony Torrini. I'm a prosecuting attorney in New Jersey investigating the murder of a Pete Fogel, also known as Pete Jackson."

"Yes, I'm aware of the case."

"Senator, I have several questions to ask you. I can be there in a couple of hours to take a deposition, or you can come here, if you prefer."

The senator knew leaving his office surrounded by police and investigators would make the media news stream across the country. He wanted to avoid the glaring lights, the microphones thrust in the face, the unforgiving cameras that caught every damaging facial expression.

"I'll come there, later this morning," Joe said. "I'm bringing my lawyer, Jack Kaiser, with me."

• • •

The two arrived at the prosecutor's office by rental car, casually dressed to be as inconspicuous as possible. Torrini extended his hand for a shake; so did his deputy prosecutor and two police investigators.

"Thank you for coming, senator. Would you like some coffee?"

160

"No, water will be fine."

The deputy prosecutor filled a cup at the water cooler and placed it in front of Joe, then sat down at an imposing oval table.

"I spoke with an Officer Steve Rainey from the police department about an accident report, a fender-bender that occurred on the night of Pete's murder. We have a witness who swears that he saw your car get hit by a driver who was leaving Bucky's bar, on Leech Street. He wrote down the license-plate number, went back into the bar, asked around and, when no one claimed the car, gave the number to the bartender, who called the police the next day. Do you affirm that it was your car?"

"Yes, it was mine."

"Did you drive it there?"

"Yes."

"Earlier you told police you were not in New Jersey that night. Did you lie?"

"I was afraid, confused. I did park my car there."

"Tell us what you did after that."

"I planned on going to the pizza place where Pete wanted to meet, but I had too much to drink and decided to sleep it off."

"What time was this?"

"I'm not sure, but I think it was before nine."

"Is that why he contacted you? To meet with him?"

"Yes."

"Did he threaten to expose you? Did he want money?"

161

"Of course not. There was no exposing to be done. And money had nothing to do with it. Pete found out about the girl from Ralph."

"How do you know that?"

"Pete told me about it years ago. He said Ralph was so drunk, he couldn't remember what he did that night."

"Did you talk to Pete on a regular basis?"

"No, only a couple of times through the years."

"Have you ever given money to Pete, for any reason?"

"I've helped Pete out of a few minor scrapes with the law, but I never gave him money."

"Did he pay you for your help?"

"No."

"You help him out, and he doesn't pay you anything? That doesn't sound like gratefulness to me."

"Pete had a lot of problems, always did. He didn't have any money, so I helped him pro bono."

"How did you know where it was you were to meet him?"

"He called me."

"Oh, when you said he got your answering machine?"

Joe rubbed his forehead and emitted a deep sigh. "I said I didn't talk to him because I didn't want to get involved."

One of the officers probed with a few questions of his own.

"After you left Bucky's, where did you go to 'sleep it off?'"

"I don't know Plainfield. I just pulled off into a

parking lot somewhere."

"You drove your car?"

"Yes."

"But you didn't notice that someone had run into you? You didn't claim your car when the bartender asked about it?"

"No."

"Why?"

"As I said, I didn't want to be involved. This was Pete's mess."

"Did anyone see you in the parking lot?"

"No, I don't think so."

"Did you see Pete?"

"No."

"Did you take a cab anywhere?"

"No. Why would I do that?"

"We have a witness, a cab driver, who will swear that he picked you up in the parking lot of Harry's Warehouse and drove you to Pete's place some time before 9."

Chapter Nineteen

"So the Lord said to Cain, 'Why are you angry? And why has your countenance fallen? If you do well, will you not be accepted? And if you do not do well, sin lies at the door. And its desire is for you, but you should rule over it.'" Genesis 4:6-7

• • •

As news of Pete's murder, and Joe's alleged involvement, spread across Indiana and the D.C. party circuit, Joe's influence was able to keep it out of the nightly news and newspapers, particularly The Fort Observer. He decided to do some damage control by leaving Washington for Indiana and, he hoped, to explain the situation with the party faithful. This was the stickiest situation he'd ever been in, and it was the first one he would have to handle on his own, without his father's considerable money and influence.

When he was expelled in college for cheating, Dad papered things over with a truckload of money and promises of a new library wing. And when the lusty, painted women in bed threatened to expose Joe, he had a book full of their sins that would guarantee a destroyed life. No one had stopped him yet, and he was determined no one ever would.

Although Pete's letter was highly damaging, it was, after all, a letter written by a man of dubious history, a felon, a possible blackmailer and one of questionable, even disreputable, character.

Joe was certain he could contain the damage and come out on top again. He thought of the trips and trinkets, the meals and lodgings, the vacations at rich donors' homes and the kickback money he had taken from those with expensive suits and conniving minds. No one could touch him, no one has yet, and he has one of the best lawyers on the hill.

• • •

He decided to meet with Kate, to explain his side of things. He knew he could; he always could. He was handsome, intelligent, well-dressed, urbane. He had respect; he had power. If he sometimes felt he didn't have love, it wasn't an overarching need. To Joe, power and respect were the high-octane elements that kept his life running. Those who needed love, or even to be liked, were weak, needy, ineffectual. No one who knew Joe would ever make such silly assessments about him. He had what he wanted, what he needed.

Kate was just entering her apartment when the phone rang. She tossed her coat and darted to reach it. When she picked up the receiver, she recognized the self-possessed voice, never failing in its charm.

"Uncle Joe," she said apprehensively, then felt embarrassed by the lack of familiarity that once came so naturally to her.

"Kate, I think we need to talk. I'm in the city, and I want to give you my side of a complicated matter. I know you have questions, and I have answers. Please give me a chance to explain."

"I do have a lot of questions."

"And I will answer them. I have a dinner date, but could we meet around 9:00 p.m., on the Riverwalk near Manini's?

"I'll be there."

• • •

A white slice of moon glistened on the dark, corrugated waters, meshing with the luminous city lights in a peaceful, moving montage of earth, city and water. Kate pulled her coat collar up when a breeze chilled her arms as the two strolled the city's Riverwalk.

Joe was unusually introspective, discussing Vietnam, the years before his senate win, his ambitions and hopes.

"I want you to better understand the time your father and I lived in," he said. "It was pretty crazy. President Kennedy was assassinated; Martin Luther King was assassinated; Bobby Kennedy was assassinated; President Johnson escalated the war. Its brutality flooded the nightly news; it was in magazine photos and everywhere. College campuses were cauldrons of unrest and anger — the kids were against the war and every tradition thrust upon them from the time they were in diapers. Charlie Manson recruited his clan of murderers, comprised of the disaffected, messed up, drugged out. Haight-Ashbury was the place to be. Timothy Leary espoused 'tune in, turn on, drop out.' The cliché was 'make love, not war.' Fathers and sons were at war with each other. Parents were appalled by

167

the openly sexual behavior of their children. Woodstock was a drugged-out love-in, with kids from all over the country writhing in mud, sweat, urine and human feces.

"We were all trying to find ourselves in the midst of chaos — in the world and in ourselves. It all seemed upside down; everything we thought was right wasn't, and everything we thought was wrong, well, sometimes it didn't seem to be so."

His lofty meanderings halted; he stopped walking and contemplated his next words. He turned to Kate; his face reflected a darkness she had never before seen.

"We were all so young, so full of life, so confident of our own invincibility. But we also were confused, impulsive, immature. We were trapped in a war we couldn't win, and we were hated when we got home; we were called 'baby killers' and worse. The chant was 'Hey, hey, LBJ, how many kids did you kill today?' The war had left its mark, on all of us. And when we got back, well, we weren't welcomed, respected, honored. Some vets were drug-addicted or alcoholics — or both. Jobs were hard to find. Stressed out? We were told to deal with it, get over it.

"And me? I worked hard to get over it."

Joe's voice dropped to a whisper, a soliloquy that resonated in the hollow places of his mind.

"I never remember a time when I didn't want to make my mark on the world, to be noticed, revered, a part of the movers and shakers of this world. And I wanted to be remembered, not just by my family or my

168

grandchildren. I wanted the world to note who I was, what I accomplished with my life. I wanted to go down in history books. Hell, I wanted to be president — the greatest president — remembered for ending poverty, bringing peace, saving the world from its own destruction.

"I hoped my war record would pave the way to that end, but it ended up being a liability. I was forced to renounce my service in Vietnam, join forces against the war, become a member of the peace movement. My ambition was so overwhelming, I couldn't see any other path to win."

Kate eyes were bored on his.

"What did you do to achieve that win? What did you do?"

"I did what I had to do."

"And what was that?"

Joe sighed, a deep, tired reflex that encompassed the emptiness in his soul.

"I-I didn't plan to kill Pete," he said. "It was just a terrible accident."

"An accident?"

"Pete was trying to blackmail me, to blackmail all of us, because of what he did in Vietnam. He wouldn't take responsibility. His whole life was a mess."

Kate scoped the concrete sidewalk, its lines, wrinkles, spaces, searching for the right words.

"I, um, I had a talk with someone who was with the prosecutor, who put me in touch with Pete's sister, Sally.

A letter was found in a safe box, one written by Pete, uh, to his sister. She read it to me."

"What did it say?"

"I think you probably know. Essentially, it said that you killed the girl, the one in Vietnam. Pete caught you, but you threatened to expose his drug dealings. And to keep him quiet throughout the years, you've given him money and legal help."

Joe reared his head, his disdain emanating in a sputtered little laugh.

"If I gave him money, he wouldn't have been living in that shithouse he called home. Okay, so I helped him out of a few scrapes with the law. Isn't that what buddies do?"

"Do buddies have each other killed?"

"What do you mean?" Joe's hand jerked nervously as he placed it in his pocket.

"Pete said you had him kill my father. He also said he didn't know it was my father he killed until he read about it the next day."

"Pete's a liar. Now I know he was nuts. Why in God's name would I kill your father? He was my friend, my buddy, my best employee even. What possible reason could I have had?"

"My father was investigating the death of that girl; Tom begged him to find the truth. Perhaps you listened in on their conversation on another phone line — I don't know. But you knew what Tom wanted, and I'm quite certain you figured out why Tom was so desperate to meet with my father."

Joe looked obliquely at the lights in the buildings, his heavy-lidded eyes dead to the evening glow that illuminated their empty spaces. City sounds, horns braying, loud music from a distant bar intruded on the awkward silence.

"Is the letter true?"

The responsive voice was sepulchral, other-worldly in its hollowness.

"I didn't mean for things to end up this way."

A stunned silence allowed Joe to continue with his stream of consciousness.

"I didn't want to kill Pete. I just wanted to keep him quiet. Pete was a lost soul. What good would it do to dredge up ancient history? To bring down a sitting senator? Don't you see? I just wanted all of this to go away."

"What was your part in my father's death?"

"I liked Pat; he was a good man, but he didn't understand how life works, how the game is played. He was always so concerned about 'doing the right thing.' He viewed the world in good and evil, black and white, never comprehending the difficult nuances of moral comprehension and survival that play a role in what we do, how we behave.

"The world is a charade of smoke and mirrors, multiple shades of gray. There are no absolute rights or wrongs; there's no strict moral compass that we all must follow in lockstep.

171

"Patrick was one of the smartest men I've ever known, but he was so simplistic in his approach to life. The deed was done; why did he have to resurrect it?"

"So you killed the girl, then killed my father for investigating it?"

"It isn't that simple, Kate. You sound like your father. We each find our own truths, inside of us. There's no concrete archetype that doesn't bend with the circumstances or change with the times. Please, try to understand the gradations, the nuances, of living, of surviving, for God's sake!"

A well of rage exploded from Kate, hot and vengeful in its force. She lunged at Joe with her hands clenched.

"How could you?" she screeched, pounding on his chest. "Why? Why?" Her arms flailed wildly to make contact. "I trusted you! I cared for you! I respected you! My father did, too! Why?"

Joe grabbed her arms so tightly that her wrists began to go numb.

"Try to understand!" he said. "You must understand! I-I had things I had to do! I had a plan! I couldn't just throw it all away! The girl was dead; don't you understand? What good would it do to bring it all up again?

His voice weakened, just a little. "I didn't want to hurt your father; I didn't want to hurt anybody. I just —, I —, I had things I had to do!"

"And everyone else is a mere pawn in that plan of yours? Expendable as yesterday's garbage? You had things to do, so everyone else has to play along, and if they get in the way, you kill them?"

"No, that's not it. You're twisting my words!"

Joe released his grip, pushed Kate away and wiped the sweat from his face with the back of his hand. "You're just like the others. You don't understand.

"I'm a senator," his voice cracked. "I do good things, great things, for this country. I build schools and hospitals, highways and bridges! I help families, children! I work hard! I'm a good person!"

"Good people don't spill innocent human blood! Good people don't look at the rest of the world like an insignificant chess game, with all the pieces scrambling about to do their bidding!"

Joe's eyes narrowed; his mouth was hard and set. He pulled the revolver from his pocket, glinting against the moon's shard of light, hard and cold and deadly. He held the gun askance, as if wondering what to do with it and who to shoot. And then his voice spoke again, ghastly and morbid.

"I have no choice but to end things this way."

A third voice, from the shadows, ordered "Drop the gun."

Though the voice was stern, Kate knew immediately whose it was.

"I said, drop it."

Joe spied his adversary as the voice took on human form. Carefully, he bent his knees and placed the revolver on the concrete.

173

Tri retrieved the gun and pointed it at Joe.

"Take a good look," the voice said. "Take a good, long look at the brother of Phi Nhung Nguyen, the Vietnamese girl you murdered."

"Tri!" Kate shrieked.

Joe looked at Tri with the dullness of incomprehension. Cold sweat beaded on his forehead like tiny air bubbles.

"You. Your sister was —"

"My sister was a young girl with a full life ahead of her. My sister was a baby, and you murdered her! And now, I will take the pleasure of murdering you!"

"Wait. Wait," Joe stammered. "I can do things for you, give you things — money —"

"We are all pawns in your chess game, aren't we?" Tri said. "But this time, it's a checkmate."

"Tri, don't do it," Kate implored. Her feelings were rife with hate and rage and furious, murderous desires. Why was she saying this?

"Don't, Tri!"

Tri edgily balanced the gun in both hands, aiming at Joe's heart. But his short hesitation gave Joe the opportunity to sweep his left arm across the barrel, pointing it upward. The two struggled, the gun pointed left, then right, then up, but Joe was heavier. He seized the gun and held it as Tri recoiled.

Joe knew he could kill Tri with ease, but he would have to kill Kate, too. He would probably be arrested for Pete's murder; certainly, the rest would be discovered. But he understood this was no fork in the

174

road; this was a dead end with a towering wall 100 feet high that blocked all light, all hope, all escape.

His trembling hand gripped the gun with ferocity as Kate and Tri watched the barrel move from their sight to Joe's right temple.

"No!" Kate cried.

The crack of the gun reverberated across the waters of the St. Jude River as Joe's limp body slammed on the concrete sidewalk, his bloody face mottled and disfigured in the eerie glare of streetlights.

After a stunned silence, Kate gingerly knelt to check his pulse.

"He's dead," she said.

She could not stem the deluge of tears, brought by years of missing a beloved father, a life with him destroyed, the betrayal of someone she cared for, so much pain, so much death, so much loss.

Tri and Kate embraced, briefly, to comfort each other. Joe was dead, they knew, but it was not over. The hardest part was before them — the part that compels living anew, laughing again, finding joy in lives that have been so anguishingly rent.

Chapter Twenty

"Though nothing can bring back the hour
Of splendour in the grass, of glory in the flower;
We will grieve not, rather find
Strength in what remains behind."
William Wordsworth

• • •

Kate and Tri understood the intertwining of their lives
— the separation and loss they experienced. They were
orphaned, stranded islands near the sweet earth of
those who belong to others, those who are woven into
the fabric of the human race as sisters, brothers, mothers,
fathers, children, cousins — relatives, kinfolk, blood.

Observing the comings and goings of those who laugh
and talk and eat with la familia exposed a deep, hollow
well in Kate. Her holidays now were small, quiet
gatherings with friends, pleasant enough, but lacking in
the robust milk of mirth and merriment and yes, so
much noise and confusion a person could get lost in
them.

• • •

For Tri, the hardness of his soul, that steely resolve —
his intrepid companion — now became the stumbling
block that hindered him from breathing the deep peace
of God's love.

Buddhism, the faith of his family, does not understand
the concept of sin. One must earn one's righteousness

and eliminate all worldly desire. It is centered on the universality of suffering and a fatalism of life that cannot be denied. It is knowledge, conduct, self-denial and meditation that lead to the fruits of life's enlightenment. But Buddhism, and Christianity, can be twisted and reconciled as one's mind chooses to have it.

Although Tri's father considered himself a Buddhist, he had killed the young boy who sullied his daughter, then he killed himself. Tri never spoke of his father's suicide to anyone, preferring instead to let everyone assume he was a war casualty.

But on the night of October 23, 1969, Tri's world was unalterably changed. He could not have imagined how many more lives would also be changed — and ended — by that one murderous act.

Never driven by materialism, Tri's sole purpose was to avenge his sister's death, and his father's death, too, when he was brutally honest with himself. Now that purpose, that man, was dead. Tri did not dwell on how he would take this man's life. He only knew he would, he must, find the guilty one. After that, his life had no meaning. Tri had no family, and his life was destroyed by a man who took away the pleasure of killing him. What would be his enlightenment now?

• • •

Kate found it was difficult to sort what feelings impelled her most — her heartsickness over the murder of her beloved father, or the fury that entwined her heart, and sucked joy and laughter and deep contentment from her life. She worked daily to fight the demons that clutched at her, who often drew her into a tornado of hatred and rage. At other times, she was better able to keep the devils at bay, wade through serene waters and feel her soul restored.

How did her father forgive God, she wondered, when her mother died. Emily's passing could not be blamed on human frailty such as selfishness, greed or even carelessness. It was clearly the hand of God — giving and taking away. How does one forgive God? If one dislikes the hand he is dealt, can he blame the dealer? Does shaking one's angry fist at God prove to be, in the dwelling house of life, an act that leads to love, joy and a thankful existence?

She wanted to better understand, to look through this dark glass. And she implored God to give her insight, strength and, yes, even acceptance, because the ghouls returned daily, and the straitjacket constraining her heart allowed little room for restoration.

• • •

Although Ben had not experienced the tragic events that enveloped her life, he had become a friend, a confidante, a comforter even. His solid temperament and empathetic heart shone through his numerous talks with Kate. He realized he was in love with her but, right now, she needed a friend, a true friend, and he was thankful to be that.

• • •

179

"(God's) peace is like a shaft of golden Light shining on you continuously." Sarah Young, "Jesus Calling."

• • •

"And ultimately forgiveness is a gift of grace rather than an act of will. I have to be willing to forgive, but I cannot will myself to forgive. I can forgive with my mind, but forgiveness is finally a matter of the heart. And the forgiveness of the heart comes from God, not from me. My part in it is to be willing to accept it. One test which indicates whether or not forgiveness has really taken place is to look at whatever it is that needs to be forgiven and see if it still hurts. If it does, forgiveness has not yet happened. But I have also learned, and I have learned it through pain, that I must be patient with myself. Just as my body is going to need more time to complete its healing from the physical trauma of the accident, so my heart, my spirit, also need time, and I, ever impatient, must be patient with myself."
Madeleine L'Engle

• • •

Thumbing through her father's Bible, Kate discovered a bookmarked page, its edges tattered from overuse, and read from the Psalm her father boldly outlined in red ink: "Out of the depths I cry to you, Lord; Lord, hear my voice. Let Your ears be attentive to my cry for mercy. If You, Lord, kept a record of sins, Lord, who could stand?

"But with You there is forgiveness, so that we can, with reverence, serve You. I wait for the Lord, my whole being waits, and in His word I put my hope. I wait for the Lord more than watchmen wait for the morning, more than watchmen wait for the morning. Israel, put your hope in the Lord, for with the Lord is unfailing love and with Him is full redemption." (Psalm 130:1-7)

Through the tears that blurred her vision and moistened her face, Kate knew she could not let rage and bitterness clutch her heart and bloody her soul. She had to forgive for her sake, not because a stern God had ordered her to. She wanted the freedom, the peace, the deep joy that can come only by letting go of the destructive forces that keep our hearts and minds closed. She imagined herself unclenching her hand, opening it to the rays of God's light, allowing Him to take the hate and hurt and baptize her with the soul-still waters that comfort.

She deeply desired the loving kindness of God, to be in His company, to walk with Him through all of life and then, to dwell with Him forever.

She would never really understand, not in this world anyway, why God allows such cruelty and pain to happen, especially to His people, but she decided, daily, that she would wait for the Lord, resting in His comforting arms until her stay on this earth has ended. And when the fires of rage burned inside her, she would open the book with the red-inked Psalm and quell the fierce tempests with the peace of God's grace, the peace that passes all understanding.

FORGIVENESS

By George Roemisch

Forgiveness is the wind-blown bud
which blooms in placid beauty at Verdun.
Forgiveness is the tiny slate-gray sparrow
which has built its nest of twigs
and string among the shards of glass
upon the wall of shame.
Forgiveness is the child who laughs
in merry ecstasy beneath the toothed fence
that closes in Da Nang.
Forgiveness is the fragrance
of the violet which still clings fast
to the heel that crushed it.
Forgiveness is the broken dream
which hides itself within the corner of the mind
oft called forgetfulness so that
it will not bring pain to the dreamer.
Forgiveness is the reed which stands up
straight and green when nature's
mighty rampage halts, full spent.
Forgiveness is a God Who will not leave us
after all we've done.

ABOUT THE AUTHOR

Fort Wayne, Indiana, native Donna Volmerding has worked as a writer and editor since 1986. She started out writing articles for a local newspaper, *The News-Sentinel*, then was hired as an editor on a national magazine. When the magazine moved out of state, she became a newspaper editor — editing, designing and laying out a monthly newspaper from her home office. She has held this job since 1988.

During this time, she also worked for several years as a copy editor and reporter at *The News-Sentinel*. She has been published in magazines, newspapers and other publications.

The Fragrance of Mercy is her first book, and she prays that there will be many more.

You can read more of Donna's thoughts and opinions on her blog — ptft.blogspot.com.

Made in the USA
Lexington, KY
15 September 2019